CW00343486

DUMB WAITER:
The war was over, but nobody had bothered to tell the machines...

THE FUNERAL:
It was quite a ceremony; after all, it was a world that had died...

THE SLICED-CROSSWISE ONLY-ON-TUESDAY WORLD:
Man could travel between the stars, but not between the Days...

GOODLIFE:
The Starship was as ancient as Time itself, but it still remembered its mission: DESTROY MAN!

THE DUSTY ZEBRA:
There are certain problems involved in setting up an inter-dimensional trading post...

NOBODY'S HOME:
The children are tired of chasing the sun. They want cruelty, glory and dirt...

ALPHA 4

By The Same Author

ALPHA 6
ALPHA 8
HAWKSBILL STATION
TO LIVE AGAIN
TO OPEN THE SKY
EPOCH
(ed. by Roger Elwood and Robert Silverberg)

ALPHA 9

EDITED BY

ROBERT SILVERBERG

A BERKLEY BOOK
published by
BERKLEY PUBLISHING CORPORATION

Copyright © 1978, by Robert Silverberg

All rights reserved

Published by arrangement with the author's agent

All rights reserved which includes the right
to reproduce this book or portions thereof in
any form whatsoever. For information address

Berkley Publishing Corporation
200 Madison Avenue
New York, New York 10016

SBN 425-03838-6

BERKLEY MEDALLION BOOKS are published by
Berkley Publishing Corporation
200 Madison Avenue
New York, N.Y. 10016

BERKLEY MEDALLION BOOK ® TM 757,375

Printed in the United States of America

Berkley Edition, October, 1978

ACKNOWLEDGMENTS

"Dumb Waiter," by Walter M. Miller, Jr. Copyright 1952 by Walter M. Miller, Jr. Reprinted by permission of Harold Matson Co., Inc.

"The Monsters," by Robert Sheckley. Copyright 1953 by Fantasy House, Inc. Reprinted by permission of the author and his agent, Sterling Lord.

"The Sliced-Crosswise Only-on-Tuesday World," by Philip José Farmer. Copyright © 1971 by Robert Silverberg. Reprinted by permission of the author and his agents, Scott Meredith Literary Agency, Inc.

"The Funeral," by Kate Wilhelm. Copyright © 1972 by Harlan Ellison. Reprinted by permission of the author.

"The Book," by Michael Shaara. Copyright 1953 by Galaxy Publishing Corporation. Reprinted by permission of the author.

"Dusty Zebra," by Clifford D. Simak. Copyright 1954 by Galaxy Publishing Corporation. Reprinted by permission of the author and his agent, Robert P. Mills, Ltd.

"Goodlife," by Fred Saberhagen. Copyright © 1963 by Galaxy Publishing Corporation. Reprinted by permission of the author and his agents, Scott Meredith Literary Agency, Inc.

"Nobody's Home," by Joanna Russ. Copyright © 1972 by Robert Silverberg. Reprinted by permission of the author.

CONTENTS

INTRODUCTION

The ALPHA series—now in its ninth year—has by now become an eight-inch shelf of the best in short science-fiction stories. Our editorial bias is doggedly middle-of-the-road, or so we like to think; that is, I try to avoid the worst excesses of the avant-garde on the one hand, and the blast-and-slash foolishness of pulp adventure fiction on the other. Of course, one reader's traditional and staid is another's wild experimentalism—very likely the fans of Hugo Gernsback's pioneering *Amazing Stories* of the 1920's muttered angrily in their soup over the gaudy innovations of John Campbell's *Astounding Science Fiction* in 1939—and so the best I can do is provide an annual sampler of the sort of science fiction that pleases *me,* that defines by example what *I* think science fiction ought to be, and hope that others will agree.

As before, this year's collection is centered heavily in the 1950's, when the average level of literary accomplishment in the science-fiction magazines finally reached some sort of parity with the quality of the thinking behind the stories, and there are representatives of the 1960's and 1970's on hand as well to provide a more rounded picture of the growth in narrative vigor of the science-fiction short story. What continues to surprise me, as I sift through the archives for material for these collections, is the inexhaustibility of the supply. Such a treasury of bright, sparkling, imaginative fiction! I hope to go on rummaging through it for years to come—for my delight and, I trust, for yours.

—Robert Silverberg

DUMB WAITER

by Walter M. Miller, Jr.

Some science-fiction writers remain active and vigorously creative through careers spanning many decades—Williamson, Simak, Heinlein, and van Vogt are four names that come quickly to mind—and some, like Walter M. Miller, Jr., whirl quickly through our midst like passing meteors, leaving dazzling trails behind. Miller's first science-fiction story, "Secret of the Death Dome," appeared in the January, 1951 *Amazing Stories,* and by 1957 he had ceased to publish, for reasons unknown to me. His gifts to the world of science fiction include one imperishable novel, *A Canticle for Leibowitz,* and about two dozen sturdy, sinewy shorter works. This one, 1952's "Dumb Waiter," is typical—a clear-eyed vision of the computerized society that was only a dream when the story was written, and which is virtually upon us now, a quarter of a century later.

ALPHA 9

He came riding a battered bicycle down the bullet-scarred highway that wound among the hills, and he whistled a tortuous flight of the blues. Hot August sunlight glistened on his forehead and sparkled in droplets that collected in his week's growth of blond beard. He wore faded khaki trousers and a ragged shirt, but his clothing was no shabbier than that of the other occasional travelers on the road. His eyes were half closed against the glare of the road, and his head swayed listlessly to the rhythm of the melancholy song. Distant artillery was rumbling gloomily, and there were black flecks of smoke in the northern sky. The young cyclist watched with only casual interest.

The bombers came out of the east. The ram-jet fighters thundered upward from the outskirts of the city. They charged, spitting steel teeth and coughing rockets at the bombers. The sky snarled and slashed at itself. The bombers came on in waves, occasionally loosing an earthward trail of black smoke. The bombers leveled and opened their bays. The bays yawned down at the city. The bombers aimed. Releases clicked. No bombs fell. The bombers closed their bays and turned away to go home. The fighters followed them for a time, then returned to land. The big guns fell silent. And the sky began cleaning away the dusky smoke.

The young cyclist rode on toward the city, still whistling the blues. An occasional pedestrian had stopped to watch the battle.

"You'd think they'd learn someday," growled a chubby man at the side of the road. "You'd think they'd know they didn't drop anything. Don't they realize they're out of bombs?"

"They're only machines, Edward," said a plump lady who stood beside him. "How can they know?"

"Well, they're supposed to think. They're supposed to be able to learn."

The voices faded as he left them behind. Some of the wanderers who had been walking toward the city now turned around and walked the other way. Urbanophiles looked at the city and became urbanophobes. Occasionally a wanderer who had gone all the way to the outskirts came trudging back. Occasionally a phobe stopped a phile and they talked. Usually the phile became a phobe and they both walked away together. As the young man moved on, the traffic became almost nonexistent. Several travelers warned him back, but he continued stubbornly. He had come a long way. He meant to

2

return to the city. Permanently.

He met an old lady on top of a hill. She sat in an antique chair in the center of the highway, staring north. The chair was light and fragile, of hand-carved cherry wood. A knitting bag lay in the road beside her. She was muttering softly to herself: "Crazy machines! War's over. Crazy machines! Can't quit fightin'. Somebody oughta—"

He cleared his throat softly as he pushed his bicycle up beside her. She looked at him sharply with haggard eyes set in a seamy mask.

"Hi!" he called, grinning at her.

She studied him irritably for a moment. "Who're you, boy?"

"Name's Mitch Laskell, Grandmaw. Hop on behind. I'll give you a ride."

"Hm-m-m! I'm going t'other way. You will, too, if y'got any sense."

Mitch shook his head firmly. "I've been going the other way too long. I'm going back, to stay."

"To the city? Haw! You're crazier than them machines."

His face fell thoughtful. He kicked at the bike pedal and stared at the ground. "You're right, Grandmaw."

"Right?"

"Machines—they aren't crazy. It's just people."

"Go on!" she snorted. She popped her false teeth back in her mouth and chomped them in place. She hooked withered hands on her knees and pulled herself wearily erect. She hoisted the antique chair lightly to her shoulder and shuffled slowly away toward the south.

Mitch watched her and marveled at the tenacity of life. Then he resumed his northward journey along the trash-littered road where motor vehicles no longer moved. But the gusts of wind brought faint traffic noises from the direction of the city, and he smiled. The sound was like music, a deep-throated whisper of the city's song.

There was a man watching his approach from the next hill. He sat on an apple crate by the side of the road, and a shotgun lay casually across his knees. He was a big, red-faced man, wearing a sweat-soaked undershirt, and in the sun his eyes were narrowed to slits. He peered fixedly at the approaching cyclist, then came slowly to his feet and stood as if blocking the way.

"Hi, fellow," he grunted.

Mitch stopped and gave him a friendly nod while he mopped his face with a kerchief. But he eyed the shotgun suspiciously.

"If this is a stickup—"

The big man laughed. "Naw, no heist. Just want to talk to you a minute. I'm Frank Ferris." He offered a burly paw.

"Mitch Laskell."

They shook hands gingerly and studied each other.

"Why you heading north, Laskell?"

"Going to the city."

"The planes are still fighting. You know that?"

"Yeah. I know they've run out of bombs, too."

"You know the city's still making the Geigers click?"

Mitch frowned irritably. "What *is* this? There can't be much radioactivity left. It's been three years since they scattered the dust. I'm not corn-fed, Ferris. The half-life of that dust is five months. It should be less than one per cent—"

The big man chuckled. "Okay, you win. But the city's not safe anyhow. The Central Computer's still at work."

"So what?"

"Ever think what would happen to a city if every ordinance was kept in force after the people cleared out?"

Mitch hesitated, then nodded. "I see. Thanks for the warning." He started away.

Frank Ferris caught the handlebars in a big hand. "Hold on!" he snapped. "I ain't finished talking."

The smaller man glanced at the shotgun and swallowed his anger.

"Maybe your audience isn't interested, Buster," he said with quiet contempt.

"You will be. Just simmer down and listen!"

"I don't hear anything."

Ferris glowered at him. "I'm recruitin' for the Sugarton crowd, Laskell. We need good men."

"Count me out. I'm a wreck."

"Cut the cute stuff, boy! This is serious. We've got two dozen men now. We need twice that many. When we get them we'll go into the city and dynamite the Computer installations. Then we can start cleaning it up."

"Dynamite? *Why?*" Mitch Laskell's face slowly gathered angry color.

"So people can live in it, of course. So we can search for food without having a dozen mechanical cops jump us when we break into a store."

"How much did Central cost?" Mitch asked stiffly. It was a rhetorical question.

Ferris shook his head irritably. "What does that matter now? Money's no good anyway. You can't sell Central for junk. Heh, heh! Wake up, boy!"

The cyclist swallowed hard. A jaw muscle tightened in his cheek, but his voice came calmly.

"You help build Central, Ferris? You help design her?"

"Wh-why, no! What kind of a question is that?"

"You know anything about her? What makes her work? How she's rigged to control all the subunits? You know that?"

"No, I—"

"You got any idea about how much sweat dripped on the drafting boards before they got her plans drawn? How many engineers slaved over her, and cussed her, and got drunk when their piece of the job was done?"

Ferris was sneering faintly. "You *know*, huh?"

"Yeah."

"Well that's all too bad, boy. But she's no good to anybody now. She's a hazard to life and limb. Why, you can't go inside the city without—"

"She's a machine, Ferris. An intricate machine. You don't destroy a tool just because you're finished with it for a while."

They glared at each other in the hot sunlight.

"Listen, boy—people built Central. People got the right to wreck her, too."

"I don't care about rights," Mitch snapped. "I'm talking about what's sensible, sane. But nobody's got the right to be stupid."

Ferris stiffened. "Watch your tongue, smart boy."

"I didn't ask for this conversation."

Ferris released the handlebars. "Get off the bicycle," he grunted ominously.

"Why? You want to settle it the hard way?"

"No. We're requisitioning your bicycle. You can walk from here on. The Sugarton crowd needs transportation. We need good men, but I guess you ain't one. Start walking."

Mitch hesitated briefly. Then he shrugged and dismounted on the side away from Ferris. The big man held the shotgun cradled lazily across one forearm. He watched Mitch with a mocking grin.

Mitch grasped the handlebars tightly and suddenly rammed the front wheel between Ferris's legs. The fender made a tearing sound. The shotgun exploded skyward as the big man fell back. He sat down screaming and doubling over. The gun clattered into the road. He groped for it with a frenzied hand. Mitch kicked him in the face and a tooth slashed at his toe through the boot leather. Ferris fell aside, his mouth spitting blood and white fragments.

Mitch retrieved the shotgun and helped himself to a dozen shells from the other's pockets, then mounted the bicycle and pedaled away. When he had gone half a mile, a rifle slug spanged off the pavement beside him. Looking back, he saw three tiny figures standing beside Ferris in the distance. The "Sugarton crowd" had come to take care of their own, no doubt. He pedaled hard to get out of range, but they wasted no more ammunition.

He realized uneasily that he might meet them again if they came to the city intending to sabotage Central. And Ferris wouldn't miss a chance to kill him, if the chance came. Mitch didn't believe he was really hurt, but he was badly humiliated. And for some time to come he would dream of pleasant ways to murder Mitch Laskell.

Mitch no longer whistled as he rode along the deserted highway toward the sun-drenched skyline in the distance. To a man born and bred to the tune of mechanical thunder, amid vistas of concrete and steel, the skyline looked good—looked good even with several of the buildings twisted into ugly wreckage. It had been dusted in the radiological attack, but not badly bombed. Its defenses had been more than adequately provided for—which was understandable, since it was the capital and the legislators appropriated freely.

It seemed unreasonable to him that Central was still working. Why hadn't some group of engineers made their way into the main power vaults to kill the circuits temporarily? Then he remembered that the vaults were self-defending and that there were probably very few technicians left who knew how to handle the job. Technicians had a way of inhabiting industrial regions, and wars had a way of destroying those regions. Dirt farmers usually had the best survival value.

Mitch had been working with aircraft computers before he became displaced, but a city's Central Service Coordinator was a far cry from a robot pilot. Centrals weren't built all at once; they grew over a period of years. At first, small units were set up in power plants and waterworks to regulate voltages and flows and circuit conditions automatically. Small units replaced switchboards in telephone exchanges. Small computers measured traffic flow and regulated lights and speed limits accordingly. Small computers handled bookkeeping where large amounts of money were exchanged. A computer checked books in and out at the library, also assessing the fines. Computers operated the city buses and eventually drove most of the routine traffic.

That was the way the city's Central Service grew. As more computers were assigned to various tasks, engineers were hired to coordinate them, to link them with special circuits and to set up central "data tanks," so that a traffic regulator in the north end would be aware of traffic conditions in the main thoroughfares to the south. Then, when the micro-learner relay was invented, the engineers built a central unit to be used in conjunction with the central data tanks. With the learning units in operation, Central was able to perform most of the city's routine tasks without attention from human supervisors.

The system had worked well. Apparently it was still working well three years after the inhabitants had fled before the chatter of the Geiger counters. In one sense Ferris had been right: A city whose machines carried on as if nothing had happened—that city might be a dangerous place for a lone wanderer.

But dynamite certainly wasn't the answer, Mitch thought. Most of man's machinery was already wrecked or lying idle. Humanity had waited a hundred thousand years before deciding to build a technological civilization. If it wrecked this one completely, it might never build another.

Some men thought that a return to the soil was desirable. Some men tried to pin their guilt on the machines, to lay their own stupidity on the head of a mechanical scapegoat and absolve themselves with dynamite. But Mitch Laskell was a man who liked the feel of a wrench and a soldering iron—liked it better than the feel of even the most well-balanced stone ax or wooden plow. And he liked the purr of a pint-sized nuclear engine much better than the braying of a harnessed jackass.

He was willing to kill Frank Ferris or any other man who sought to wreck what little remained. But gloom settled over him as he thought, "If everybody decides to tear it down, what can *I* do to stop it?" For that matter, would he then be right in trying to stop it?

At sundown he came to the limits of the city, and he stopped just short of the outskirts. Three blocks away a robot cop rolled about in the center of the intersection, rolled on tricycle wheels while he directed the thin trickle of traffic with candy-striped arms and with "eyes" that changed color like a stoplight. His body was like an oil drum, painted fire-engine red. The head, however, had been cast in a human mold, with a remarkably Irish face and a perpetual predatory smile. A short radar antenna grew from the center of his head, and the radar was his link with Central.

Mitch sat watching him with a nostalgic smile, even though he knew such cops might give him considerable trouble once he entered the city. The "skaters" were incapable of winking at petty violations of ordinance.

As the daylight faded, photronic cells notified Central, and the streetlights winked on promptly. A moment later, a car without a taillight whisked by the policeman's corner. A siren wailed in the policeman's belly. He skated away in hot pursuit, charging like a mechanical bull. The car screeched to a stop. "O'Reilly" wrote out a ticket and offered it to any empty back seat. When no one took it, the cop fed it into a slot in his belly, memorized the car's license number, and came clattering back to his intersection, where the traffic had automatically begun obeying the ordinances governing nonpoliced intersections.

The cars were empty, computer-piloted. Their destinations were the same as when they had driven regular daily routes for human passengers: salesmen calling on regular customers, inspectors making their rounds, taxis prowling their assigned service areas.

Mitch Laskell stood shivering. The city sounded sleepy but alive. The city moved and grumbled. But as far as he could see down the wide boulevard, no human figure was visible. The city was depopulated. There was a Geiger on a nearby lamppost. It clucked idly through a loudspeaker. But it indicated no danger. The city should be radiologically safe.

But after staring for a long time at the weirdly active streets, Mitch muttered, "It'll wait for tomorrow."

He turned onto a side road that led through a residential district just outside the city limits. Central's jurisdiction did not extend here, except for providing water and lights. He meant to spend the night in a deserted house, then enter the city at dawn.

Here and there a light burned in one of the houses, indicating that he was not alone in his desire to return. But the pavement was scattered with rusty shrapnel, with fragments fallen from the sky battles that still continued. Even by streetlight he could see that some of the roofs were damaged. Even though the bombers came without bombs, there was still danger from falling debris and from fire. Most former city dwellers who were still alive preferred to remain in the country.

Once he passed a house from which music floated softly into the street, and he paused to listen. The music was scratchy—a worn record. When the piece was finished there was a moment of silence, and the player played it again—the last record on the stack, repeating itself. Otherwise the house was still.

Mitch frowned, sensing some kind of trouble. He wheeled the bicycle toward the curb, meaning to investigate.

"I live there," said a woman's voice from the shadows.

She had been standing under a tree that overhung the sidewalk, and she came slowly out into the streetlight. She was a dark, slender girl with haunted eyes, and she was holding a baby in her arms.

"Why don't you turn off your record player?" he asked. "Or change to the other side?"

"My husband's in there," she told him. "He's listening to it. He's been listening to it for a long time. His name is George. Why don't you go say hello to him?"

Mitch felt vaguely disturbed. There was a peculiar note in the girl's quiet Spanish accent. Still, he wanted to talk to someone who had ventured into the city. He nodded and smiled at the girl.

"I'd like to."

"You just go on in. I'll stay out here. The baby needs fresh air."

He thanked her and strolled up on the porch. The record player stopped, tried to change, and played the same piece again. Mitch knocked once. Hearing no answer, he entered and moved along the hallway toward the light in the kitchen. But suddenly he stopped.

The house smelled musty. And it smelled of something else. Many times he had smelled the syrup-and-stale-fish odor of death. He advanced another step toward the kitchen.

He saw a porcelain-topped table. He saw a hand lying across the table. The hand was bloated, lying amid brown stains that also covered the forearm and sleeve. The hand had dropped a butcher knife.

"Dead several days," he thought—and backed away.

He turned the record player off as he left the house. The girl was standing at the curb gazing down at his bicycle. She glanced at him amiably and spoke.

"I'm glad you turned that record off, George. A man just came by and wanted to know why you played it so often. You must have been asleep."

Mitch started. He moistened his lips and stared at her wonderingly. "I'm not—" He feel silent for a moment, then stuttered, "You haven't been in the house?"

"Yes, but you were asleep in the kitchen. Did the man come talk to you?"

"Look, I'm not—" He choked and said nothing. The dark-eyed baby was eyeing him suspiciously. He lifted the bicycle and swung a long leg across the saddle.

"George, where are you going?"

"Just for a little ride," he managed to gasp.

"On the man's bicycle?"

Something was twisting cruelly at his insides. He stared at the girl's wide brown eyes for a moment. And then he said it. "Sure, it's all right. He's asleep—at the kitchen table."

Her mouth flickered open, and for an instant sanity threatened to return. She rocked dizzily. Then, after a deep breath, she straightened.

"Don't be gone too long, George."

"I won't! Take good care of the baby."

He pedaled away on wings of fright. For a time he cursed himself, and then he fell to cursing the husband who had taken an easy road, leaving his wife to stumble alone. Mitch wondered if he should have stayed to help her. But there was nothing to be done for her, nothing at least that was in his power to do. Any gesture of help might become an irreparable blunder. At least she still had the child.

A few blocks away he found another house with an intact roof, and he prepared to spend the night. He wheeled the bicycle into the parlor and fumbled for the lights. They came on, revealing a dusty room and furniture with frayed upholstery. He made a brief tour of the house. It had been recently occupied, but there was still unopened cans in the kitchen, and still crumpled sheets on the bed. He ate a cold supper, shaved, and prepared to retire. Tomorrow would be a dangerous day.

Sleep came slowly. Sleep was full of charging ram-jets in flak-scarred skies, full of tormented masses of people that swarmed in exodus from death-sickened cities. Sleep was full of babies wailing, and women crying in choking sobs. Sleep became white arms and soft caresses.

The wailing and sobbing had stopped. It was later. Was he awake? Or still asleep? He was warm, basking in a golden glow, steeped in quiet pleasure. Something—something was there, something that breathed.

"What—!"

"*Sshhh!*" purred a quiet voice. "Don't say anything."

Some of the warmth fled before a sudden shiver. He opened his eyes. The room was full of blackness. He shook his head dizzily and stuttered.

"*Sshhh!*" she whispered again.

"What is this?" he gasped. "How did you get—?"

"Be quiet, George. You'll wake the baby."

He sank back in utter bewilderment, with winter frosts gathering along his spine.

Night was dreamlike. And dawn came, washing the shadows with grayness. He opened his eyes briefly and went back to sleep. When he opened them again, sunlight was flooding the room.

He sat up. *He was alone.* Of course! It had only been a dream.

He muttered irritably as he dressed. Then he wandered to the kitchen for breakfast.

Warm biscuits waiting in the oven! The table was set! There was a note on his plate. He read it and slowly flushed.

> There's jam in the cupboard, and I hope you like the biscuits. I know he's dead. Now I think I can go on alone. Thanks for the shotgun and bicycle. Marta.

He bellowed a curse and charged into the parlor. The bike was gone. He darted to the bedroom. The shotgun was gone. He ran shouting to the porch, but the street was empty.

Sparrows fluttered about the eaves. The skyline of the business district lay lonesome in the morning sun. Squirrels were rustling in the branches of the trees. He looked at the weedy lawns where no children played, the doors askew on their hinges, at a bit of aircraft wreckage jutting from the roof of a fire-gutted home—the rotting porches—the emptiness.

He rubbed his cheek ruefully. It was no world for a young mother and her baby. The baby would fit nicely in the bicycle's basket. The shotgun would offer some protection against the human wolf packs that prowled everywhere these days.

"Little thief!" he growled halfheartedly.

But when the human animal would no longer steal to protect its offspring, then its prospects for survival would be bleak indeed. He shrugged gloomily and wandered back to the kitchen. He sat down and ate the expensive biscuits—and decided that George couldn't have cut his throat for culinary reasons. Marta was a good cook.

He entered the city on foot and unarmed, later in the morning.

He chose the alleyways, avoiding the thoroughfares where traffic purred and where the robot cops enforced the letter of the law. At each corner he paused to glance in both directions for possible mechanical observers before darting across the open street to the next alley. The Geigers on the lampposts were clicking faster as he progressed deeper into the city, and twice he paused to inspect the readings of their integrating dials. The radioactivity was not yet dangerous, but it was higher than he had anticipated. Perhaps it had been dusted again after the exodus.

He stopped to prowl through an empty house and an empty garage. He came out with a flashlight, a box of tools, and a crowbar. He had no certain plan, but tools would be needed if he meant to call a temporary halt to Central's activities. It was dangerous to enter any building, however; Central would call it burglary, unless the prowler could show legitimate reason for entering. He needed some kind of identification.

After an hour's search through several houses in the residential district, he found a billfold containing a union card and a pass to several restricted buildings in the downtown area. The billfold belonged to a Willie Jesser, an air-conditioning and refrigeration mechanic for the Howard Cooler Company. He pocketed it after a moment's hesitation. It might not be enough to satisfy Central, but for the time being it would have to do.

By early afternoon he had reached the beginnings of the commercial area. Still he had seen no signs of human life. The thinly scattered traffic moved smoothly along the streets, carrying no passengers. Once he saw a group of robot climbers working high on a telephone pole. Some of the telephone cables carried the coordinating circuits for the city's network of computers. He detoured several blocks to avoid them and wandered on glumly. He began to realize that he was wandering aimlessly.

The siren came suddenly from half a block away. Mitch stopped in the center of the street and glanced fearfully toward it. A robot cop was rolling toward him at twenty miles an hour! He broke into a run.

"You will halt, please!" croaked the cop's mechanical voice. "The pedestrian with the toolbox will please halt!"

Mitch stopped at the curb. Flight was impossible. The skater could whisk along at forty miles an hour if he chose.

The cop's steel wheels screeched to a stop a yard away. The head nodded a polite but jerky greeting. Mitch stared at the creature's eyes, even though he knew the eyes were duds; the cop was seeing him by the heat waves from his bodily warmth, and touching him with a delicate aura of radar.

"You are charged with jaywalking, sir. I must present you with a summons. Your identification, please."

Mitch nervously produced the billfold and extracted the cards. The cop accepted them in a pair of tweezerlike fingers and instantly memorized the information.

"This is insufficient identification. Have you nothing else?"

"That's all I have with me. What's wrong with it?"

"The pass and the union card expired in 1987."

Mitch swallowed hard and said nothing. He had been afraid of this. Now he might be picked up for vagrancy.

"I shall consult Central Coordinator for instructions," croaked the cop. "One moment, please."

A dynamotor purred softly in the policeman's cylindrical body. Then Mitch heard the faint twittering of computer code as

13

the cop's radio spoke to Central. There was a silence lasting several seconds. Then an answer twittered back. Still the cop said nothing. But he extracted a summons form from a pad, inserted it in a slot in his chassis, and made chomping sounds like a small typesetter. When he pulled the ticket out again, it was neatly printed with a summons for Willie Jesser to appear before Traffic Court on July 29, 1989. The charge was jaywalking.

Mitch accepted it with bewilderment. "I believe I have a right to ask for an explanation," he muttered.

The cop nodded crisply. "Central Service units are required to furnish explanations of decisions when such explanations are demanded."

"Then why did Central regard my identification as sufficient?"

"Pause for translation of Central's message," said the cop. He stood for a moment, making burring and clicking sounds. Then: "Referring to arrest of Willie Jesser by unit Six-Baker. Do not book for investigation. Previous investigations have revealed no identification papers dated later than May 1987 in the possession of any human pedestrian. Data based on one hundred sample cases. Tentative generalization by Central Service: It has become impossible for humans to produce satisfactory identification. Therefore, 'satisfactory identification' is temporarily redefined, pending instruction from authorized human legislative agency."

Mitch nodded thoughtfully. The decision indicated that Central was still capable of "learning," of gathering data and making generalizations about it. But the difficulty was still apparent. She was allowed to act on such generalizations only in certain very minor matters. Although she might very well realize the situation in the city, she could do nothing about it without authority from an authorized agency. That agency was a department of the city government, currently nonexistent.

The cop croaked a courteous, "Good day, sir!" and skated smoothly back to his intersection.

Mitch stared at his summons for a moment. The date was still four days away. If he weren't out of the city by then, he might find himself in the lockup, since he had no money to pay a fine.

Reassured now that his borrowed identity gave him a certain amount of safety, he began walking along the sidewalks instead of using the alleys. Still, he knew that Central was observing him through a thousand eyes. Counters on every corner were set to record the passage of pedestrian traffic and to relay the information to Central, thus helping to avoid congestion. But Mitch *was* the pedestrian traffic. And the counters clocked his passage. Since the data were available to the logic units, Central might make some unpleasant deductions about his presence in the city.

Brazenness, he decided, was probably the safest course to steer. He stopped at the next intersection and called to another mechanical cop, requesting directions to City Hall.

But the cop paused before answering, paused to speak with Central, and Mitch suddenly regretted his question. The cop came skating slowly to the curb.

"Six blocks west and four blocks north, sir," croaked the cop. "Central requests the following information, which you may refuse to furnish if you so desire: As a resident of the city, how is it that you do not know the way to City Hall, Mr. Jesser?"

Mitch whitened and stuttered nervously, "Why, I've been gone three years. I . . . I had forgotten."

The cop relayed the information, then nodded. "Central thanks you. Data have been recorded."

"Wait," Mitch muttered. "Is there a direct contact with Central in City Hall?"

"Affirmative."

"I want to speak to Central. May I use it?"

The computer code twittered briefly. "Negative. You are not listed among the city's authorized computer personnel. Central suggests you use the Public Information Unit, also in City Hall, ground floor rotunda."

Grumbling to himself, Mitch wandered away. The P.I.U. was better than nothing, but if he had access to the direct service contact, perhaps to some extent he could have altered Central's rigid behavior pattern. The P.I.U. however would be well guarded.

A few minutes later he was standing in the center of the main lobby of the City Hall. The great building had suffered some damage during an air raid, and one wing was charred by fire. But the rest of it was still alive with the rattle of machinery. A headless servo-secretary came rolling past him, carrying a trayful of pink envelopes. Delinquent utility bills, he guessed.

Central would keep sending them out, but of course human authority would be needed to suspend service to the delinquent customers. The servo-secretary deposited the envelopes in a mailbox by the door, then rolled quickly back to its office.

Mitch looked around the gloomy rotunda. There was a desk at the far wall. Recessed in a panel behind the desk were a microphone, a loudspeaker, and the lens of a television camera. A sign hung over the desk, indicating that here was the place to complain about utility bills, garbage-disposal service, taxes, and inaccurate weather forecasts. A citizen could also request any information contained in Central Data except information relating to defense or to police records.

Mitch crossed the rotunda and sat at the desk facing the panel. A light came on overhead. The speaker crackled for a moment.

"Your name, please?" it asked.

"Willie Jesser."

"What do you wish from Information Service, please?"

"A direct contact with Central Data."

"You have a screened contact with Central Data. Unauthorized personnel are not permitted an unrestricted contact, for security reasons. Your contact must be monitored by this unit."

Mitch shrugged. It was as he had expected. Central Data was listening and speaking, but the automatics of the P.I.U. would be censoring the exchange.

"All right," he grumbled. "Tell me this: Is Central aware that the city has been abandoned? That its population is gone?"

"Screening, screening, screening," said the unit. "Question relates to civil defense."

"Is Central aware that her services are now interfering with human interests?"

There was a brief pause. "Is this question in the nature of a complaint?"

"Yes," he grated acidly. "It's a complaint."

"About your utility services, Mr. Jesser?"

Mitch spat an angry curse. "About all services!" he bellowed. "Central has got to suspend all operations until new ordinances are fed into Data."

"That will be impossible, sir."

"Why?"

16

"There is no authorization from Department of City Services."

He slapped the desk and groaned. "There *is* no such department now! There is no city government! The city is abandoned!"

The speaker was silent.

"Well?" he snapped.

"Screening," said the machine.

"Listen," he hissed. "Are you screening what I say, or are you just blocking Central's reply?"

There was a pause. "Your statements are being recorded in Central Data. Replies to certain questions must be blocked for security reasons."

"The war is over!"

"Screening."

"You're trying to maintain a civil status quo that went out of existence three years ago. Can't you use your logic units to correct present conditions?"

"The degree of self-adjustment permitted to Central Service is limited by ordinance number—"

"Never mind!"

"Is there anything else?"

"Yes! What will you do when fifty men come marching in to dynamite the vaults and destroy Central Data?"

"Destroying city property is punishable by a fine of—"

Mitch cursed softly and listened to the voice reading the applicable ordinance.

"Well, they're planning to do it anyway," he snapped.

"Conspiracy to destroy city property is punishable by—"

Mitch stood up and walked away in disgust. But he had taken perhaps ten steps when a pair of robot guards came skating out from their wall niches to intercept him.

"One moment sir," they croaked in unison.

"Well?"

"Central wishes to question you in connection with the alleged conspiracy to destroy city property. You are free to refuse. However, if you refuse, and if such a conspiracy is shown to exist, you may be charged with complicity. Will you accompany us to Interrogation?"

A step closer to jail, he thought gloomily. But what was there to lose? He grunted assent and accompanied the skaters out the entrance, down an inclined ramp, and past a group of heavily barred windows. They entered the police court, where a booking computer clicked behind its desk. Several servo-secretaries and robot cops were waiting quietly for task assignments.

Mitch stopped suddenly. His escorts waited politely.

"Will you come with us, please?"

He stood staring around at the big room—at the various doorways, one leading to traffic court, and at the iron gate to the cellblock.

"I hear a woman crying," he muttered.

The guards offered no comment.

"Is someone locked in a cell?"

"We are not permitted to answer."

"Suppose I wanted to go bail," he snapped. "I have a right to know."

"You may aske the booking desk whether a specific individual is being held. But generalized information cannot be released."

Mitch strode to the booking computer. "Are you holding a woman in jail?"

"Screening."

It was only a vague suspicion, but he said, "A woman named Marta."

"Full name, please."

"I don't know it. Can't you tell me?".

"Screening."

"Listen! I loaned my bicycle to a woman named Marta. If you have the bicycle, I want it!"

"License number, please."

"A 1987 license—number six zero five zero."

"Check with Lost and Found, please."

Mitch controlled himself slowly. "Look—*you* check. I'll wait."

The computer paused. "A bicycle with that license number has been impounded. Can you produce proof of ownership?"

"*On a bicycle*? I knew the number. Isn't that enough?"

"Describe it, please?"

Mitch described it wearily. He began to understand Ferris's desire to retire Central permanently and forcibly. At the moment he longed to convert several subcomputers to scrap metal.

"Then," said the speaker, "if vehicle is yours, you may have it by applying for a new license and paying the required fee."

"Refer that to Central Data," Mitch groaned.

The booking computer paused to confer with the Coordinator. "Decision stands, sir."

"But there aren't any new licenses!" he growled. "A while ago Central said— Oh, never mind!"

"That decision applied to identification, sir. This applies to licensing of vehicles. Insufficient data have been gathered to permit generalization."

"Sure, sure. All right, what do I do to get the girl out of jail?"

There was another conference with the Coordinator, then: "She is being held for investigation. She may not be released for seventy-two hours."

Mitch dropped the toolbox that he had been carrying since morning. With a savage curse he rammed the crowbar through a vent in the device's front panel and slashed it about in the opening. There was a crash of shattering glass and a shower of sparks. Mitch yelped at the electric jolt and lurched away. Steel fingers clutched his wrists.

Five minutes later he was being led through the gate to the cellblocks, charged with maliciously destroying city property; and he cursed himself for a hot-tempered fool. They would hold him until a grand jury convened, which would probably be never.

The girl's sobbing grew louder as he was led along the iron corridors toward a cell. He passed three cells and glanced inside. The cells were occupied by dead men's bones. *Why?* The rear wall was badly cracked, and bits of loose masonry were scattered on the floor. Had they died of concussion during an attack? Or been gassed to death?

They led him to the fifth cell and unlocked the door. Mitch stared inside and grinned. The rear wall had been partially wrecked by a bomb blast, and there was room to crawl through the opening to the street. The partition that separated the adjoining cell was also damaged, and he caught a glimpse of a white, frightened face peering through the hole. Marta.

He glanced at his captors. They were pushing him gently through the door. Evidently Central's talents did not extend to bricklaying, and she could not judge that the cell was less than escapeproof.

The door clanged shut behind him.

"Marta," he called.

Her face had disappeared from the opening. There was no answer.

"Marta."

"Let me alone," grumbled a muffled voice.

"I'm not angry about the bicycle."

He walked to the hole and peered through the partition into the next cell. She crouched in a corner, peering at him with frightened, tear-reddened eyes. He glanced at the opening in the rear wall.

"Why haven't you gone outside?" he asked.

She giggled hysterically. "Why don't you go look down?"

He stepped to the opening and glanced twenty feet down to a concrete sidewalk. He went back to stare at the girl.

"Where's your baby?"

"They took him away," she whimpered.

Mitch frowned and thought about it for a moment. "To the city nursery, probably—while you're in jail."

"They won't take care of him! They'll let him die!"

"Don't scream like that. He'll be all right."

"Robots don't give milk!"

"No, but there are such things as bottles, you know," he chuckled.

"Are there?" Her eyes were wide with horror. "And what will they put in the bottles?"

"Why—" He paused. Central certainly wasn't running any dairy farms.

"Wait'll they bring you a meal," she said. "You'll see."

"Meal?"

"Empty tray," she hissed. "Empty tray, empty paper cup, paper fork, clean paper napkin. No food."

Mitch swallowed hard. Central's logic was sometimes hard to see. The servo-attendants probably went through the motions of ladling stew from an empty pot and drawing coffee from an empty urn. Of course, there weren't any truck farmers to keep the city supplied with produce.

"So that's why...the bones...in the other cells," he muttered.

"They'll starve us to death!"

"Don't scream so. We'll get out. All we need is something to climb down on."

"There isn't any bedding."

"There's our clothing. We can plait a rope. And if necessary we can risk a jump."

She shook her head dully and stared at her hands. "It's no use. They'd catch us again."

Mitch sat down to think. There was bound to be a police arsenal somewhere in the building, probably in the basement. The robot cops were always unarmed. But of course there had been a human organization for investigation purposes and to assume command in the event of violence. When one of the traffic units faced a threat, it could do nothing but try to handcuff the offender and call for human help. There were arms in the building somewhere, and a well-placed rifle shot could penetrate the thin sheet-steel bodies.

He deplored the thought of destroying any of the city's service machinery, but if it became necessary to wreck a few subunits, it would have to be done. He must somehow get access to the vaults where the central data tanks and the coordinators were located—get to them before Ferris's gang came to wreck them completely, so that they might be free to pick the city clean.

An hour later he heard the cellblock gate groan open, and he arose quickly. Interrogation, he thought. They were coming to question him about the plot to wreck Central. He paused to make a hasty decision, then scrambled for the narrow opening and clambered through it into the adjoining cell while the skater came rolling down the corridor.

The girl's eyes widened. "Wh-what are you—"

"*Shhh!*" he hissed. "This might work."

The skater halted before his cell while he crouched against the wall beyond the opening.

"Willie Jesser, please," the robot croaked.

There was silence. He heard the door swing open. The robot rolled around inside his cell for a few seconds, repeating his name and brushing rubble aside to make way. If only he failed to look through the opening!

Suddenly a siren growled and the robot went tearing down the corridor again. Mitch stole a quick glance. The robot had left the door ajar. He dragged the girl to her feet and snapped, "Let's go."

They squeezed through the hole and raced out into the corridor. The cellblock gate was closed. The girl moaned weakly. There was no place to hide.

The door bolts were operated from remote boxes placed in the corridor so as to be beyond the reach of the inmates. Mitch dragged the girl quickly toward another cell, opened the control panel, and threw the bolt. He closed the panel, leaving the bolt open. They slipped quickly inside the new cell, and he pulled the door quietly closed. The girl made a choking sound as she stumbled over the remains of a former inmate.

"Lie down in the corner," he hissed, "and keep still. They're coming back in force."

"What if they notice the bolt is open?"

"Then we're sunk. But they'll be busy down at our end of the hall. Now shut up."

They rolled under the steel cot and lay scarcely breathing. The robot was returning with others. The faint twitter of computer code echoed through the cellblocks. Then the skaters rushed past and screeched to a stop before the escapee's cell. He heard them enter. He crawled to the door for a look, then pushed it open and stole outside.

He beckoned the girl to his side and whispered briefly. Then they darted down the corridor on tiptoe toward the investigators. They turned as he raced into view. He seized the bars and jerked the door shut. The bolt snapped in place as Marta tugged at the remote.

Three metal bodies crashed simultaneously against the door and rebounded. One of them spun around three times before recovering.

"Release the lock, please."

Mitch grinned through the bars. "Why don't you try the hole in the wall?"

The robot who had spun crazily away from the door now turned. He went charging across the cell floor at full acceleration—and sailed out wildly into space.

An ear-splitting crash came from the street. Shattered metal skidded across pavement. A siren wailed and brakes shrieked. The others went to look—and began twittering.

Then they turned. "You will surrender, please. We have summoned armed guards to seize you if you resist."

Mitch laughed and tugged at the whimpering girl.

"Wh-where—?"

"To the gate. Come on."

They raced swiftly along the corridor. And the gate was opening to admit the "armed guards." But of course no human bluecoats charged through. The girl muttered in frightened bewilderment, and he explained on the run.

"Enforced habit pattern. Central has to do it, even when no guards are available."

Two repair units were at work on the damaged booking computer as the escapees raced past. The repair units paused, twittered a notation to Central, then continued with their work.

Minutes later they found the arsenal, and the mechanical attendant had set out a pair of .45's for the "armed guards." Mitch caught up one of them and fired at the attendant's sheet-metal belly. The robot careened crazily against the wall, emitted a shower of blue sparks, and stood humming while the metal around the hole grew cherry red. There was a dull cough. The machine smoked and fell silent.

Mitch vaulted across the counter and caught a pair of submachine guns from the rack. But the girl backed away, shaking her head.

"I couldn't even use your shotgun," she panted.

He shrugged and laid it aside. "Carry as much ammunition as you can, then," he barked.

Alarm bells were clanging continuously as they raced out of the arsenal, and a loudspeaker was thundering a request for all human personnel to be alert and assist in their capture. Marta was staggering against him as they burst out of the building into the street. He pushed her back against the wall and fired a burst at two skaters who raced toward them down the sidewalk. One crashed into a fireplug; the other went over the curb and fell in the street.

"To the parking lot!" he called over his shoulder.

But the girl had slumped in a heap on the sidewalk. He grumbled a curse and hurried to her side. She was semiconscious, but her face was white and drawn. She shivered uncontrollably.

"What's wrong?" he snapped.

There was no answer. Fright had dazed her. Her lips moved, seemed to frame a soundless word: "George."

Muttering angrily, Mitch stuffed a fifty-round drum of

23

ammunition in his belt, took another between his teeth, and lifted the girl over one shoulder. He turned in time to fire a one-handed burst at another skater. The burst went wide. But the skater stopped. Then the skater ran away.

He gasped and stared after it. The blare of the loudspeaker was furnishing the answer.

". . . All human personnel. Central patrol service has reached the limit of permissible subunit expenditure. Responsibility for capture no longer applies without further orders to expend subunits. Please instruct. Commissioner of Police, please instruct. Waiting. Waiting."

Mitch grinned. Carrying the girl, he stumbled toward a car on the parking lot. He dumped her in the back seat and started in behind her, but a loudspeaker in the front protested.

"Unauthorized personnel. This is Mayor Sarquist's car. Unauthorized personnel. Please use an extra."

Mitch looked around. There were no extras on the lot. And if there had been one, it would refuse to carry him unless he could identify himself as authorized to use it.

Mayor Sarquist's car began twittering a radio protest to Central. Mitch climbed inside and wrenched loose the cable that fed the antenna. The loudspeaker began barking complaints about sabotage. Mitch found a toolbox under the back seat and removed several of the pilot-computer's panels. He tugged a wire loose, and the speaker ceased complaining. He ripped at another, and a bank of tubes went dead.

He drove away, using a set of dial controls for steering. The girl in the back seat began to recover her wits. She sat up and stared out the window at the thin traffic. The sun was sinking and the great city was immersing itself in gloom.

"You're worthless!" he growled at Marta. "The world takes a poke at you, and you jump into your mental coffin and nail the lid shut. How do you expect to take care of your baby?"

She continued to stare gloomily out the window. She said nothing. The car screeched around a corner, narrowly missing a mechanical cop. The cop skated after them for three blocks, siren wailing; then it abandoned the chase.

"You're one of the machine age's spoiled children," he fumed. "Technologists gave you everything you could possibly want. Push a button, and you get it. Instead of taking part in the machine age, you let it wait on you. You spoiled yourself. When

24

the machine age cracks up, you crack up, too. Because you never made yourself its master; you just let yourself be mechanically pampered."

She seemed not to hear him. He swung around another corner and pulled to the curb. They were in front of a three-story brick building set in the center of a green-lawned block and surrounded by a high iron fence. The girl stared at it for a moment and raised her chin slowly from her fist.

"The city orphanage!" she cried suddenly and bounded outside. She raced across the sidewalk and beat at the iron gate with her fists.

Mitch climbed out calmly and opened it for her. She darted up toward the porch, but a servo-attendant came rolling out to intercept her. Its handcuff hand was open to grasp her wrist.

"*Drop low!*" he bellowed at her.

She crouched on the walkway, then rolled quickly aside on the lawn. A burst of machine-gun fire brightened the twilight. The robot spun crazily and stopped, hissing and sputtering. Wrecking a robot could be dangerous. If a bullet struck the tiny nuclear reactor just right, there would be an explosion.

They skirted wide around it and hurried into the building. Somewhere upstairs a baby was crying. A servo-nurse sat behind a desk in the hall, and she greeted them as if they were guests.

"Good evening, sir and madam. You wish to see one of the children?"

Marta started toward the stairs, but Mitch seized her arm. "No! Let *me* go up. It won't be pretty."

But she tore herself free with a snarl and bounded up the steps toward the cry of her child. Mitch shrugged to himself and waited. The robot nurse protested the illegal entry but did nothing about it.

"Noooo—!"

A horrified shriek from the girl! He glanced up the staircase, knowing what was wrong but unable to help her. A moment later he heard her vomiting. He waited.

A few minutes later she came staggering down the stairway, sobbing and clutching her baby tightly against her. She stared at Mitch with tear-drenched eyes, gave him a wild shake of her head, and babbled hysterically.

"Those cribs! They're full of little bones. Little bones—all over the floor. Little bones—"

"Shut up!" he snapped. "Be thankful yours is all right. Now let's get out of here."

After disposing of another robotic interferer they reached the car, and Mitch drove rapidly toward the outskirts. The girl's sobbing ceased, and she purred a little unsung lullaby to her child, cuddling it as if it had just returned from the dead. Remorse picked dully at Mitch's heart, for having growled at her. Motherwise, she was still a good animal, despite her lack of success in adjusting to the reality of a ruptured world.

"Marta—?"

"What?"

"You're not fit to take care of yourself."

He said it gently. She only stared at him as he piloted the car.

"You ought to find a big husky gal who wants a baby, and let her take care of it for you."

"No."

"It's just a suggestion. None of my business. You want your baby to live, don't you?"

"George promised he'd take care of us. George always took care of us."

"George killed himself."

She uttered a little whimper. "Why did he do it? Why? I went to look for food. I came back, and there he was. Why, *why*?"

"Possibly because he was just like you. What did he do—before the war?"

"Interior decorator. He was good, a real artist."

"Yeah."

"Why do you say it *that* way? He *was*."

"Was he qualified to live in a mechanical culture?"

"I don't know what you mean."

"I mean—could he control his slice of mechanical civilization, or did it control him?"

"I don't see—"

"Was he a button-pusher and a switch-puller? Or did he care what made the buttons and switches work? Men misuse their tools because they don't understand the principles of the tools. A man who doesn't know how a watch works might try to fix it with a hammer. If the watch is communal property, he's got no right to fool with it. A nontechnologist has no right to take part in a technological civilization. He's a bull in a china shop. That's what happened to our era. Politicians were given powerful tools. They failed to understand the tools. They wrecked our culture with them."

"You'd have a scientist in the White House?"

"If all men were given a broad technical education, there could be nothing else there, could there?"

"Technocracy—"

"No. Simply a matter of education."

"People aren't smart enough."

"You mean they don't *care* enough. Any man above the level of a dullard has enough sense to grasp the principles of physics and basic engineering and mechanics. They just aren't motivated to grasp them. The brain is a tool, not a garbage can for oddments of information! Your baby there—he should learn the principles of logic and semantics before he's ten. He should be taught *how to use* the tool, the brain. We've just begun to learn how to think. If the common man were trained in scientific reasoning methods, we'd solve our problems in a hurry."

"What has this got to do with us?"

"Everything. Your George folded up because he couldn't control his slice of civilization and he couldn't live without it. He couldn't fix the broken toy, but he suffered from its loss. And you're in the same fix. I haven't decided yet whether you're crazy or just neurotic."

She gave him an icy stare. "Let me know when you figure it out."

They were leaving the city, driving out through the suburbs again into the night-shrouded residential areas. He drove by streetlight, for the car—accustomed to piloting itself by radar—had no headlights. Mitch thought gloomily that he had blundered. He had stalked into the city without a plan and had accomplished nothing. He had alerted Central and had managed to get himself classified as a criminal in the central data tanks. Instead of simplifying his task, he had made things harder for himself.

Whenever they passed a cop at an intersection, the cop retreated to the curb and called Central to inform the Coordinator of their position. But no attempt was made to arrest the fugitives. Having reached her limit of subunit expenditures,

Central was relying on the nonexistent human police force.

"Mayor Sarquist's house," the girl muttered suddenly.

"Huh? Where?"

"Just ahead. The big cut-stone house on the right—with part of the roof caved in."

Mitch twisted a dial in the heart of the pilot-computer, and the car screeched to a stop at the curb. The girl lurched forward.

"You woke the baby," she complained. "Why stop here? We're still in the city limits."

"I don't know," he murmured, staring thoughtfully at the dark hulk of the two-story mansion set in a nest of oaks. "Just sort of a hunch."

There was a long silence while Mitch chewed his lip and frowned at the house.

"I hear a telephone ringing," she said.

"Central calling Mayor Sarquist. You can't tell. It might have been ringing for three years."

She was looking out the rear window. "Mitch—?"

"Huh?"

"There's a cop at the intersection."

He seemed not to hear her. He opened the door. "Let's go inside. I want to look around. Bring the gun."

They strolled slowly up the walkway toward the damaged and deserted house. The wind was breathing in the oaks, and the porch creaked loudly beneath their feet. The door was still locked. Mitch kicked the glass out of a window, and they slipped into an immense living room. He found the light.

"The cop'll hear that noise," she muttered, glancing at the broken glass.

The noisy clatter of the steel-wheeled skater answered her. The cop was coming to investigate. Mitch ignored the sound and began prowling through the house. The phone was still ringing, but he could not answer it without knowing Sarquist's personal identifying code.

The girl called suddenly from the library. "What's this thing, Mitch?"

"What thing?" he yelled.

"Typewriter keyboard, but no type. Just a bunch of wires and a screen."

His jaw fell agape. He trotted quickly toward the library.

"A direct channel to the data tanks!" he gasped, staring at the metal wall panel with its encoders and the keyboard.

"What's it doing here?"

He thought about it briefly. "Must be . . . I remember: just before the exodus, they gave Sarquist emergency powers in the defense setup. He could requisition whatever was needed for civil defense—draft workers for first aid, traffic direction, and so on. He had the power to draft anybody or anything during an air raid."

Mitch aproached the keyboard slowly. He closed the main power switch, and the tubes came alive. He sat down and typed:
Central from Sarquist: You will completely clear the ordinance section of your data tanks and await revised ordinances. The entire city code is hereby repealed.

He waited. Nothing happened. There was no acknowledgment. The typed letters had not even appeared on the screen.

"Broken?" asked the girl.

"Maybe," Mitch grunted. "Maybe not. I think I know."

The mechanical cop had lowered his retractable sprockets, climbed the porch steps, and was hammering at the door. "Mayor Sarquist, please!" he was calling. "Mayor Sarquist, please!"

There was a mahogany desk, several easy chairs, a solid wall of books, and a large safe in another wall. The safe—

"Sarquist should have some rather vital papers in there," he murmured.

"What do you want with papers?" the girl snapped. "Why don't we get out of the city while we can?"

He glanced at her coldly. "Like to go the rest of the way alone?"

She opened her mouth, closed it, and frowned. She was holding the tommy gun, and he saw it twitch slightly in her hand, as if reminding him that she didn't *have* to go alone.

He walked to the safe and idly spun the dial. "Locked," he muttered. "It'd take a good charge of T.N.T. . . . or—"

"Or what?"

"Central." He chuckled dryly. "Maybe she'll do it for us."

"Are you crazy?"

"Sure. Go unlock the door. Let the policeman in."

"No!" she barked.

Mitch snorted impatiently. "All right, then, I'll do it. Pitch me the gun."

"No!" She pointed it at him and backed away.

"Give me the gun!"

"No!"

She had laid the baby on the sofa, where it was now sleeping peacefully. Mitch sat down beside it.

"Trust your aim?"

She caught her breath. Mitch lifted the child gently into his lap.

"Give me the gun."

"You wouldn't!"

"I'll give the kid back to the cops."

She whitened and handed the weapon to him quickly. Mitch saw that the safety was on, laid the baby aside, and stood up.

"Don't look at me like that!" she said nervously.

He walked slowly toward her.

"Don't you dare *touch me!*"

He picked up a ruler from Sarquist's desk, then dived for her. A moment later she was stretched out across his lap, clawing at his legs and shrieking while he applied the ruler resoundingly. Then he dumped her on the rug, caught up the gun, and went to admit the insistent cop.

Man and machine stared at each other across the threshold. The cop radioed a visual image of Mitch to Central and got an immediate answer.

"Request you surrender immediately sir."

"Am I now charged with breaking and entering?" he asked acidly.

"Affirmative."

'You planning to arrest me?"

Again the cop consulted Central. "If you will leave the city at once, you will be granted safe passage."

Mitch lifted his brows. Here was a new twist. Central was doing some interpretation, some slight modification of ordinance. He grinned at the cop and shook his head.

"I locked Mayor Sarquist in the safe," he stated evenly.

The robot consulted Central. There was a long twittering of computer code. Then it said, "This is false information."

30

"Suit yourself, tin boy. I don't care whether you believe it or not."

Again there was a twittering of code. Then: "Stand aside, please."

Mitch stepped out of the doorway. The subunit bounced over the threshold with the aid of the four-footed sprockets and clattered hurriedly toward the library. Mitch followed, grinning to himself. Despite Central's limitless "intelligence," she was as naïve as a child.

He lounged in the doorway to watch the subunit fiddling with the dials of the safe. He motioned the girl down, and she crouched low in a corner. The tumblers clicked. There was a dull snap. The door started to swing.

"Just a minute!" Mitch barked.

The subunit paused and turned. The machine gun exploded, and the brief hail of bullets tore off the robot's antenna. Mitch lowered the gun and grinned. The cop just stood there, unable to contact Central, unable to decide. Mitch crossed the room through the drifting plaster dust and rolled the robot aside. The girl whimpered her relief and came up out of the corner.

The cop was twittering continually as it tried without success to contact the Coordinator. Mitch stared at it for a moment, then barked at the girl, "Go find some tools. Search the garage, attic, basement. I want a screwdriver, pliers, soldering iron, solder, whatever you can find."

She departed silently.

Mitch cleaned out the safe and dumped the heaps of papers, money, and securities on the desk. He began sorting them out. Among the various stacks of irrelevant records he found a copy of the original specifications for the Central Coordinator vaults, dating from the time of installation. He found blueprints of the city's network of computer circuits, linking the subunits into one. His hands became excited as he shuffled through the stacks. Here were data. Here was substance for reasonable planning.

Heretofore he had gone off half-cocked and quite naturally had met with immediate failure. No one ever won a battle by being good, pure, or ethically right, despite Galahad's claims to the contrary. Victories were won by intelligent planning, and Mitch felt ashamed of his previous impulsiveness. To work out a scheme for redirecting Central's efforts would require time.

The girl brought a boxful of assorted small tools. She set them on the floor and sat down to glower at him.

"More cops outside now," she said. "Standing and waiting. The place is surrounded."

He ignored her. Sarquist's identifying code—it had to be here somewhere.

"I tell you, we should get out of here!" she whined.

"Shut up."

Mitch occasionally plucked a paper from the stack and laid it aside while the girl watched.

"What are those?" she asked.

"Messages he typed into the unit at various times."

"What good are *they*?"

He showed her one of the slips of yellowed paper. It said: *Unit 67-BJ is retired for repairs.* A number was scrawled in one corner: 5.00326.

"So?"

"That number. It was his identifying code at the time."

"You mean it's different every day?"

"More likely, it's different every minute. The code is probably based on an equation whose independent variable is *time* and whose dependent variable is the code number."

"How silly!"

"Not at all. It's just sort of a combination lock whose combination is continuously changing. All I've got to do is find the equation that describes the change. Then I can get to Central Coordinator."

She paced restlessly while he continued the search. Half an hour later he put his head in his hands and gazed despondently at the desk top. The key to the code was not there.

"What's the matter?" she asked.

"Sarquist. I figured he'd have to write it down somewhere. Evidently he memorized it. Or else his secretary did. I didn't figure a politician even had sense enough to substitute numbers in a simple equation."

The girl walked to the bookshelf and picked out a volume. She brought it to him silently. The title was *Higher Mathematics for Engineers and Physicists*.

"So I was wrong," he grunted.

"Now what?"

He shuffled the slips of paper idly while he thought about it. "I've got eleven code numbers here, and the corresponding times when they were good. I might be able to find it empirically."

"I don't understand."

"Find an equation that gives the same eleven answers for the same eleven times, and use it to predict the code number for now."

"Will it work?"

He grinned. "There are an infinite number of equations that would give the same eleven answers for the same eleven substitutions. But it might work, if I assume that the code equation was of a simple form."

She paced restlessly while he worked at making a graph with time as the abscissa and the code numbers for ordinates. But the points were scattered across the page, and there was no connecting them with any simple sort of curve. "It almost has to be some kind of repeating function," he muttered, "something that Central could check by means of an irregular cam. The normal way for setting a code into a machine is to turn a cam by clock motor, and the height of the cam's rider is the code number for that instant."

He tried it on polar coordinates, hoping to get the shape of such a cam, but the resulting shape was too irregular to be possible, and he had no way of knowing the period of the repeating function.

"That's the craziest clock I ever saw," the girl murmured.

"What?" He looked up quickly.

"That electric wall clock. Five minutes ahead of the electric clock in the living room. But when we first came it was twenty minutes ahead."

"It's stopped, maybe."

"Look at the second hand."

The red sweep was running. Mitch stared at it for a moment, then rose slowly to his feet and walked to her side. He took the small clock down from its hook and turned it over in his hands. Then he traced the cord to the wall outlet. The plug was held in place by a bracket so that it could not be removed.

The sweep hand moved slowly, it seemed. Silently he removed the screws from the case and stared inside at the works.

Then he grunted surprise. "First clock I ever saw with elliptical gears!"

"What?"

"Look at these two gears in the train. Ellipses, mounted at the foci. That's the story. For a while the clock will run faster than the other one. Then it'll run slower." He handled it with growing excitement. "That's *it*, Marta—the key. Central must have another clock just like this one. The amount of lead or lag—in minutes—is probably the code!"

He moved quickly to the direct-contact unit. "Tell me the time on the other clock!"

She hurried into the living room and called back, "Ten-seventeen and forty seconds...forty-five...fifty—"

The other clock was leading by five and one-quarter minutes. He typed 5.250 on the keyboard. Nothing happened.

"You sure that's right?" he called.

"It's now ten-eighteen—ten...fifteen...twenty."

The clock was still slowing down. He tried 5.230, but again nothing happened. The unit refused to respond. He arose with an angry grunt and began prowling around the library. "There's something else," he muttered. "There must be a modifying factor. That clock's too obvious anyway. But what else could they be measuring together except time?"

"Is that another clock on his desk?"

"No, it's a barometer. It doesn't—"

He paused to grin. "Could be! The barometric pressure difference from the mean could easily be mechanically added or subtracted from the reading of that wacky clock. Visualize this, inside of Central: The two clock motors mounted on the same shaft, with the distance between their indicator needles as the code number. Except that the distance is modified by having a barometer rigged up to shift one of the clocks one way or the other on its axis when the pressure varies. It's simple enough."

She shook her head. Mitch took the barometer with him to the unit. The dial was calibrated in atmospheres, and the pressure was now 1.03. Surely, he thought, for simplicity's sake, there would be no other factor involved in the code. This way, Sarquist could have glanced at his watch and the wall clock and the barometer and could have known the code number with only a little mental arithmetic. The wall time minus the wrist time plus the barometer's reading.

He called to the girl again, and the lag was now a little over four minutes. He typed again. There was a sharp click as the relays worked. The screen came alive, fluttered with momentary phosphorescence, then revealed the numbers in glowing type.

"We've got it!" he yelled to Marta.

She came to sit down on the rug. "I still don't see what we've got."

"Watch!" He began typing hurriedly, and the message flashed neatly upon the screen.

CENTRAL FROM SARQUIST. CLEAR YOUR TANKS OF ALL ORDINANCE DATA, EXCEPT ORDINANCES PERTAINING TO RECORDING OF INFORMATION IN YOUR TANKS. PREPARE TO RECORD NEW DATA.

He pressed the answer button and the screen went blank, but the reply was slow to come.

"It won't work!" Marta snorted. "It knows you aren't Sarquist. The subunits in the street have seen us."

"What do you mean by 'know,' and what do you mean by 'see'? Central isn't human."

"It *knows* and it *sees*."

He nodded. "Provided you mean those words in a mechanical sense. Provided you don't imply that she *cares* what she knows and sees, except where she's required to 'care' by enforced behavior patterns—ordinances."

Then the reply began crawling across the screen. SARQUIST FROM CENTRAL. INCONSISTENT INSTRUCTIONS. ORDINANCE 36-J, PERTAINING TO THE RECORDING OF INFORMATION, STATES THAT ORDINANCE DATA MAY NOT BE TOTALLY VOIDED BY YOU EXCEPT DURING RED ALERT AIR WARNING.

"See?" the girl hissed.

DEFINE THE LIMITS OF MY AUTHORITY IN PRESENT CONDITIONS, he typed. MAY I TEMPORARILY SUSPEND SPECIFIC ORDINANCES?

YOU MAY SUSPEND SPECIFIC ORDINANCES FOR CAUSE, BUT THE CAUSE MUST BE RECORDED WITH THE ORDER OF SUSPENSION.

Mitch put on a gloating grin. READ ME THE SERIES NUMBERS OF ALL LAWS IN CRIMINAL AND TRAFFIC CODES.

The reaction was immediate. Numbers began flashing on the

screen in rapid sequence. "Write these down!" he called to the girl.

A few moments later, the flashing numbers paused. WAIT, EMERGENCY INTERRUPTION, said the screen.

Mitch frowned. The girl glanced up from her notes. "What's—"

Then it came. A dull booming roar that rattled the windows and shook the house.

"Not another raid!" she whimpered.

"It doesn't sound like—"

Letters began splashing across the screen. EMERGENCY ADVICE TO SARQUIST. MY CIVILIAN DEFENSE CO-ORDINATOR HAS BEEN DESTROYED. MY ANTIAIRCRAFT COORDINATOR HAS BEEN DESTROYED. ADVISE, PLEASE.

"What happened?"

"Frank Ferris!" he barked suddenly. "The Sugarton crowd—with their dynamite! They got into the city."

CENTRAL FROM SARQUIST, he typed. WHERE ARE THE DAMAGED COORDINATORS LOCATED?

UNDERGROUND VAULT AT MAP COORDINATES K-81.

"Outside the city," he breathed. "They haven't got to the main tanks yet. We've got a little time."

PROCEED WITH ORDINANCE LISTING, he commanded.

Half an hour later they were finished. Then he began the long task of relisting each ordinance number and typing after it: REPEALED; CITY EVACUATED.

"I hear gunshots," Marta interrupted. She went to the window to peer up and down the dimly lighted streets.

Mitch worked grimly. It would take them a couple of hours to get into the heart of the city, unless they knew how to capture a robot vehicle and make it serve them. But with enough men and enough guns, they would wreck subunits until Central withdrew. Then they could walk freely into the heart of the city and wreck the main coordinators, with a consequent cessation of all city services. Then they would be free to pillage, to make a mechanical graveyard of the city that awaited the return of man.

"They're coming down this street, I think," she called.

"Then turn out all the lights!" he snapped, "and keep quiet."

"They'll see all the cops out in the street. They'll wonder why."

He worked frantically to get all the codes out of the machine before the Sugarton crowd came past. He was destroying its duties, its habit patterns, its normal functions. When he was finished it would stand by helplessly and let Ferris's gang wreak their havoc, unless he could replace the voided ordinances with new, more practical ones.

"Aren't you finished yet?" she called. "They're a couple of blocks away. The cops have quit fighting, but the men are still shooting them."

"I'm finished now!" He began rattling the keyboard frantically.

SUPPLEMENTAL ORDINANCES: #1: THERE IS NO LIMIT OF SUBUNIT EXPENDITURE.

#2: YOU WILL NOT PHYSICALLY INJURE ANY HUMAN BEING, EXCEPT IN DEFENSE OF CENTRAL COORDINATOR UNITS.

#3: ALL MECHANICAL TRAFFIC WILL BE CLEARED FROM THE STREETS IMMEDIATELY.

#4: YOU WILL DEFEND CENTRAL COORDINATORS AT ALL COSTS.

#5: THE HUMAN LISTED IN YOUR MEMORY UNITS UNDER THE NAME 'WILLIE JESSER" WILL BE ALLOWED ACCESS TO CENTRAL DATA WITHOUT CHALLENGE.

#6: TO THE LIMIT OF YOUR ABILITY YOU WILL SET YOUR OWN TASKS IN PURSUANCE OF THE GOAL: TO KEEP THE CITY'S SERVICES INTACT AND IN GOOD REPAIR, READY FOR HUMAN USAGE.

#7: YOU WILL APPREHEND HUMANS ENGAGED IN ARSON, GRAND THEFT, OR PHYSICAL VIOLENCE AND EJECT THEM SUMMARILY FROM THE CITY.

#8: YOU WILL OFFER YOUR SERVICES TO PROTECT THE PERSON OF WILLIE JESSER—

"They're here!" shouted the girl. "They're coming up the walk!"

—AND WILL ASSIST HIM IN THE TASK OF RENOVATING THE CITY, TOGETHER WITH SUCH

PERSONS AS ARE WILLING TO HELP REBUILD.

The girl was shaking him. "They're here, I tell you!"

Mitch punched a button labeled "commit to data," and the screen went blank. He leaned back and grinned at her. There was a sound of shouting in the street, and someone was beating at the door.

Then the skaters came rolling in a tide of sound two blocks away. The shouting died, and there were several bursts of gunfire. But the skaters came on, and the shouting grew frantic.

She muttered: "Now we're in for it."

But Mitch just grinned at her and lit a cigarette. Fifty men couldn't stand for long against a couple of thousand subunits who now had no expenditure limit.

He typed one last instruction into the unit. WHEN THE PLUNDERERS ARE TAKEN PRISONER, OFFER THEM THIS CHOICE: STAY AND HELP REBUILD, OR KEEP AWAY FROM THE CITY.

From now on, there weren't going to be any nonparticipators.

Mitch closed down the unit and went out to watch the waning fight.

A bigger job was ahead.

THE MONSTERS

Robert Sheckley

There are no Sheckley stories that are less than graceful, but
this one—one of his earliest, published in 1953—always struck
me as particularly elegant. There are no superfluous words, the
narrative line is taut and neat, and the philosophical understruc-
ture of the story intersects perfectly with the action on the
surface. In short, a model of craft. It also proposes—in a playful
way, to be sure—an extravagantly science-fictional extrapola-
tion of sexual mores, Swiftian in its implacability.

It is also much fun to read.

Cordovir and Hum stood on the rocky mountaintop, watching
the new thing happen. Both felt rather good about it. It was
undoubtedly the newest thing that had happened for some time.

"By the way the sunlight glints from it," Hum said, "I'd say it is made of metal."

"I'll accept that," Cordovir said. "But what holds it up in the air?"

They both stared intently down to the valley where the new thing was happening. A pointed object was hovering over the ground. From one end of it poured a substance resembling fire.

"It's balancing on the fire," Hum said. "That should be apparent even to your old eyes."

Cordovir lifted himself higher on his thick tail, to get a better look. The object settled to the ground and the fire stopped.

"Shall we go down and have a closer look?" Hum asked.

"All right. I think we have time—wait! What day is this?"

Hum calculated silently, then said, "The fifth day of Luggat."

"Damn," Cordovir said. "I have to go home and kill my wife."

"It's a few hours before sunset," Hum said. "I think you have time to do both."

Cordovir wasn't sure. "I'd hate to be late."

"Well, then. You know how fast I am," Hum said. "If it gets late, I'll hurry back and kill her myself. How about that?"

"That's very decent of you." Cordovir thanked the younger man and together they slithered down the steep mountainside.

In front of the metal object both men halted and stood up on their tails.

"Rather bigger than I thought," Cordovir said, measuring the metal object with his eye. He estimated that it was slightly longer than their village, and almost half as wide. They crawled a circle around it, observing that the metal was tooled, presumably by human tentacles.

In the distance the smaller sun had set.

"I think we had better get back," Cordovir said, noting the cessation of light.

"*I* still have plenty of time." Hum flexed his muscles complacently.

"Yes, but a man likes to kill his own wife."

"As you wish." They started off to the village at a brisk pace.

In his house, Cordovir's wife was finishing supper. She had

her back to the door, as etiquette required. Cordovir killed her with a single flying slash of his tail, dragged her body outside, and sat down to eat.

After meal and meditation he went to the Gathering. Hum, with the impatience of youth, was already there, telling of the metal object. He probably bolted his supper, Cordovir thought with mild distaste.

After the youngster had finished, Cordovir gave his own observations. The only thing he added to Hum's account was an idea: that the metal object might contain intelligent beings.

"What makes you think so?" Mishill, another elder, asked.

"The fact that there was fire from the object as it came down," Cordovir said, "joined to the fact that the fire stopped after the object was on the ground. Some being, I contend, was responsible for turning it off."

"Not necessarily," Mishill said. The village men talked about it late into the night. Then they broke up the meeting, buried the various murdered wives, and went to their homes.

Lying in the darkness, Cordovir discovered that he hadn't made up his mind as yet about the new thing. Presuming it contained intelligent beings, would they be moral? Would they have a sense of right and wrong? Cordovir doubted it, and went to sleep.

The next morning every male in the village went to the metal object. This was proper, since the functions of males were to examine new things and to limit the female population. They formed a circle around it, speculating on what might be inside.

"I believe they will be human beings," Hum's elder brother Esktel said. Cordovir shook his entire body in disagreement.

"Monsters, more likely," he said. "If you take in account—"

"Not necessarily," Esktel said. "Consider the logic of our physical development. A single focusing eye—"

"But in the great Outside," Cordovir said, "there may be many strange races, most of them non-human. In the infinitude—"

"Still," Esktel put in, "the logic of our—"

"As I was saying," Cordovir went on, "the chance is infinitesimal that they would resemble us. Their vehicle, for example. Would we build—"

"But on strictly logical grounds," Esktel said, "you can see—"

That was the third time Cordovir had been interrupted. With a single movement of his tail he smashed Esktel against the metal object. Esktel fell to the ground, dead.

"I have often considered my brother a boor," Hum said. "What were you saying?"

But Cordovir was interrupted again. A piece of metal set in the greater piece of metal squeaked, turned and lifted, and a creature came out.

Cordovir saw at once that he had been right. The thing that crawled out of the hole was twin-tailed. It was covered to its top with something partially metal and partially hide. And its color! Cordovir shuddered.

The thing was the color of wet, flayed flesh.

All the villagers had backed away, waiting to see what the thing would do. At first it didn't do anything. It stood on the metal surface, and a bulbous object that topped its body moved from side to side. But there were no accompanying body movements to give the gesture meaning. Finally, the thing raised both tentacles and made noises.

"Do you think it's trying to communicate?" Mishill asked softly.

Three more creatures appeared in the metal hole, carrying metal sticks in their tentacles. The things made noises at each other.

"They are decidedly not human," Cordovir said firmly. "The next question is, are they moral beings?" One of the things crawled down the metal side and stood on the ground. The rest pointed their metal sticks at the ground. It seemed to be some sort of religious ceremony.

"Could anything so hideous be moral?" Cordovir asked, his hide twitching with distaste. Upon closer inspection, the creatures were more horrible than could be dreamed. The bulbous object on their bodies just might be a head, Cordovir decided, even though it was unlike any head he had ever seen. But in the middle of that head! Instead of a smooth, characterful surface was a raised ridge. Two round indentures were on either side of it, and two more knobs on either side of that. And in the lower half of the head—if such it was—a pale, reddish slash ran across. Cordovir supposed this might be considered a mouth, with some stretching of the imagination.

Nor was this all, Cordovir observed. The things were so constructed as to show the presence of bone! When they moved their limbs, it wasn't a smooth, flowing gesture, the fluid motion of human beings. Rather, it was the jerky snap of a tree limb.

"God above," Gilrig, an intermediate-age male gasped. "We should kill them and put them out of their misery!" Other men seemed to feel the same way, and the villagers flowed forward.

"Wait!" one of the youngsters shouted. "Let's communicate with them, if such is possible. They might still be moral beings. The Outside is wide, remember, and anything is possible."

Cordovir argued for immediate extermination, but the villagers stopped and discussed it among themselves. Hum, with characteristic bravado, flowed up to the thing on the ground.

"Hello," Hum said.

The thing said something.

"I can't understand it," Hum said, and started to crawl back. The creature waved its jointed tentacles—if they were tentacles—and motioned at one of the suns. He made a sound.

"Yes, it is warm, isn't it?" Hum said cheerfully.

The creature pointed at the ground, and made another sound.

"We haven't had especially good crops this year," Hum said conversationally.

The creature pointed at itself and made a sound.

"I agree," Hum said. "You're as ugly as sin."

Presently the villagers grew hungry and crawled back to the village. Hum stayed and listened to the things making noises at him, and Cordovir waited nervously for Hum.

"You know," Hum said, after he rejoined Cordovir, "I think they want to learn our language. Or want me to learn theirs."

"Don't do it," Cordovir said, glimpsing the misty edge of a great evil.

"I believe I will," Hum murmured. Together they climbed the cliffs back to the village.

That afternoon Cordovir went to the surplus female pen and formally asked a young woman if she would reign in his house for twenty-five days. Naturally, the woman accepted gratefully.

On the way home, Cordovir met Hum, going to the pen.

"Just killed my wife," Hum said, superfluously, since why else would he be going to the surplus female stock?

"Are you going back to the creatures tomorrow?" Cordovir asked.

"I might," Hum answered, "if nothing new presents itself."

"The thing to find out is if they are moral beings or monsters."

"Right," Hum said, and slithered on.

There was a Gathering that evening, after supper. All the villagers agreed that the things were non-human. Cordovir argued strenuously that their very appearance belied any possibility of humanity. Nothing so hideous could have moral standards, a sense of right and wrong, and above all, a notion of truth.

The young men didn't agree, probably because there had been a dearth of new things recently. They pointed out that the metal object was obviously a product of intelligence. Intelligence axiomatically means standards of differentiation. Differentiation implies right and wrong.

It was a delicious argument. Olgolel contradicted Arast and was killed by him. Mavrt, in an unusual fit of anger for so placid an individual, killed the three Holian brothers and was himself killed by Hum, who was feeling pettish. Even the surplus females could be heard arguing about it, in their pen in a corner of the village.

Weary and happy, the villagers went to sleep.

The next few weeks saw no end of the argument. Life went on much as usual, though. The women went out in the morning, gathered food, prepared it, and laid eggs. The eggs were taken to the surplus females to be hatched. As usual, about eight females were hatched to every male. On the twenty-fifth day of each marriage, or a little earlier, each man killed his woman and took another.

The males went down to the ship to listen to Hum learning the language; then, when that grew boring, they returned to their customary wandering through hills and forests, looking for new things.

The alien monsters stayed close to their ship, coming out only when Hum was there.

Twenty-four days after the arrival of the non-humans, Hum announced that he could communicate with them, after a fashion.

44

"They say they come from far away," Hum told the village that evening. "They say that they are bisexual, like us, and that they are humans, like us. They say there are reasons for their different appearance, but I couldn't understand that part of it."

"If we accept them as humans," Mishill said, "then everything they say is true."

The rest of the villagers shook in agreement.

"They say that they don't want to disturb our life, but would be very interested in observing it. They want to come to the village and look around."

"I see no reason why not," one of the younger men said.

"No!" Cordovir shouted. "You are letting in evil. These monsters are insidious. I believe that they are capable of—telling an untruth!" The other elders agreed, but when pressed, Cordovir had no proof to back up this vicious accusation.

"After all," Sil pointed out, "just because they look like monsters, you can't take it for granted that they think like monsters as well."

"I can," Cordovir said, but he was outvoted.

Hum went on. "They have offered me—or us, I'm not sure which, various metal objects which they say will do various things. I ignored this breach of etiquette, since I considered they didn't know any better."

Cordovir nodded. The youngster was growing up. He was showing, at long last, that he had some manners.

"They want to come to the village tomorrow."

"No!" Cordovir shouted, but the vote was against him.

"Oh, by the way," Hum said, as the meeting was breaking up. "They have several females among them. The ones with the very red mouths are females. It will be interesting to see how the males kill them. Tomorrow is the twenty-fifth day since they came."

The next day the things came to the village, crawling slowly and laboriously over the cliffs. The villagers were able to observe the extreme brittleness of their limbs, the terrible awkwardness of their motions.

"No beauty whatsoever," Cordovir muttered. "And they all look alike."

In the village the things acted without any decency. They crawled into huts and out of huts. They jabbered at the surplus female pen. They picked up eggs and examined them. They peered at the villagers through black things and shiny things.

In midafternoon, Rantan, an elder, decided it was about time he killed his woman. So he pushed the thing who was examining his hut aside and smashed his female to death.

Instantly, two of the things started jabbering at each other, hurrying out of the hut.

One had the red mouth of a female.

"He must have remembered it was time to kill his own woman," Hum observed. The villagers waited, but nothing happened.

"Perhaps," Rantan said, "perhaps he would like someone to kill her for him. It might be the custom of their land."

Without further ado Rantan slashed down the female with his tail.

The male creature made a terrible noise and pointed a metal stick at Rantan. Rantan collapsed, dead.

"That's odd," Mishill said. "I wonder if that denotes disapproval?"

The things from the metal object—eight of them—were in a tight little circle. One was holding the dead female, and the rest were pointing the metal sticks on all sides. Hum went up and asked them what was wrong.

"I don't understand," Hum said, after he spoke with them. "They used words I haven't learned. But I gather that their emotion is one of reproach."

The monsters were backing away. Another villager, deciding it was about time, killed his wife who was standing in a doorway. The group of monsters stopped and jabbered at each other. Then they motioned to Hum.

Hum's body motion was incredulous after he had talked with them.

"If I understood right," Hum said, "they are ordering us not to kill any more of our women!"

"What!" Cordovir and a dozen others shouted.

"I'll ask them again." Hum went back into conference with the monsters who were waving metal sticks in their tentacles.

"That's right," Hum said. Without further preamble he flipped his tail, throwing one of the monsters across the village square. Immediately the others began to point their sticks while retreating rapidly.

After they were gone, the villagers found that seventeen males were dead. Hum, for some reason, had been missed.

"Now will you believe me!" Cordovir shouted. "The creatures told *a deliberate untruth!* They said they wouldn't molest us and then they proceed to kill seventeen of us! Not only an amoral act—but a *concerted death effort!*"

It was almost past human understanding.

"A deliberate untruth!" Cordovir shouted the blasphemy, sick with loathing. Men rarely discussed the possibility of anyone telling an untruth.

The villagers were beside themselves with anger and revulsion, once they realized the full concept of an *untruthful* creature. And, added to that was the monsters' concerted death effort!

It was like the most horrible nightmare come true. Suddenly it became apparent that these creatures didn't kill females. Undoubtedly they allowed them to spawn unhampered. The thought of that was enough to make a strong man retch.

The surplus females broke out of their pens and, joined by the wives, demanded to know what was happening. When they were told, they were twice as indignant as the men, such being the nature of women.

"Kill them!" the surplus females roared. "Don't let them change our ways. Don't let them introduce immorality!"

"It's true," Hum said sadly. "I should have guessed it."

"They must be killed at once!" a female shouted. Being surplus, she had no name at present, but she made up for that in blazing personality.

"We women desire only to live moral, decent lives, hatching eggs in the pen until our time of marriage comes. And then twenty-five ecstatic days! How could we desire more? These monsters will destroy our way of life. They will make us as terrible as they!"

"Now do you understand?" Cordovir screamed at the men. "I warned you, I presented it to you, and you ignored me! Young men must listen to old men in time of crisis!" In his rage he killed two youngsters with a blow of his tail. The villagers applauded.

"Drive them out," Cordovir shouted. "Before they corrupt us!"

All the females rushed off to kill the monsters.

"They have death-sticks," Hum observed. "Do the females know?"

"I don't believe so," Cordovir said. He was completely calm now. "You'd better go and tell them."

"I'm tired," Hum said sulkily. "I've been translating. Why don't you go?"

"Oh, let's both go," Cordovir said, bored with the youngster's adolescent moodiness. Accompanied by half the villagers they hurried off after the females.

They overtook them on the edge of the cliff that overlooked the object. Hum explained the death-sticks while Cordovir considered the problem.

"Roll stones on them," he told the females. "Perhaps you can break the metal of the object."

The females started rolling stones down the cliffs with great energy. Some bounced off the metal of the object. Immediately, lines of red fire came from the object and females were killed. The ground shook.

"Let's move back," Cordovir said. "The females have it well in hand, and this shaky ground makes me giddy."

Together with the rest of the males they moved to a safe distance and watched the action.

Women were dying right and left, but they were reinforced by women of other villages who had heard of the menace. They were fighting for their homes now, their rights, and they were fiercer than a man could ever be. The object was throwing fire all over the cliff, but the fire helped dislodge more stones which rained down on the thing. Finally, big fires came out of one end of the metal object.

A landslide started, and the object got into the air just in time. It barely missed a mountain; then it climbed steadily, until it was a little black speck against the larger sun. And then it was gone.

That evening, it was discovered that 53 females had been killed. This was fortunate since it helped keep down the surplus female population. The problem would become even more acute now, since seventeen males were gone in a single lump.

Cordovir was feeling exceedingly proud of himself. His wife had been gloriously killed in the fighting, but he took another at once.

"We had better kill our wives sooner than every twenty-five days for a while," he said at the evening Gathering. "Just until things get back to normal."

The surviving females, back in the pen, heard him and applauded wildly.

"I wonder where the things have gone," Hum said, offering the question to the Gathering.

"Probably away to enslave some defenseless race," Cordovir said.

"Not necessarily," Mishill put in and the evening argument was on.

THE SLICED-CROSSWISE ONLY-ON-TUESDAY WORLD

Philip José Farmer

Rarely has a science-fiction writer leaped to prominence so swiftly or so spectacularly as did Philip José Farmer when his novella "The Lovers" appeared in a magazine in 1952. A brilliantly executed publicity campaign on the part of the magazine's editor helped a good deal, but hype alone could not have accounted for the impact that that strange, distinctive, and powerful story had. Richly inventive, warmly and compellingly told, and—by the standards of its era—strongly erotic, "The Lovers" was the most passionately discussed story of the year and its author became instantly famous. Nor was he a one-book phenom, either; a quarter of a century later the Farmer bibliography runs to many pages, studded with such significant novels as *Night of Light, The Maker of Universes, Image of the Beast,* and the classic *Riverworld* series. And then there are the short stories—among them "Mother" and "The Shadow of Space" from earlier numbers of *ALPHA,* and the quirky, sly, playful story with the longwinded title that we offer here.

Getting into Wednesday was almost impossible.

Tom Pym had thought about living on other days of the week. Almost everybody with any imagination did. There were even TV shows speculating on this. Tom Pym had even acted in two of these. But he had no genuine desire to move out of his own world. Then his house burned down.

This was on the last day of the eight days of spring. He awoke to look out the door at the ashes and the firemen. A man in a white asbestos suit motioned for him to stay inside. After fifteen minutes, another man in a suit gestured that it was safe. He pressed the button by the door, and it swung open. He sank down in the ashes to his ankles; they were a trifle warm under the inch-thick coat of water-soaked crust.

There was no need to ask what had happened, but he did, anyway.

The fireman said, "A short-circuit, I suppose. Actually, we don't know. It started shortly after midnight, between the time that Monday quit and we took over."

Tom Pym thought that it must be strange to be a fireman or a policeman. Their hours were so different, even though they were still limited by the walls of midnight.

By then the others were stepping out of their stoners or "coffins" as they were often called. That left sixty still occupied.

They were due for work at 08:00. The problem of getting new clothes and a place to live would have to be put off until off-hours, because the TV studio where they worked was behind in the big special it was due to put on in 144 days.

They ate breakfast at an emergency center. Tom Pym asked a grip if he knew of any place he could stay. Though the government would find one for him, it might not look very hard for a convenient place.

The grip told him about a house only six blocks from his former house. A makeup man had died, and as far as he knew the vacancy had not been filled. Tom got onto the phone at once, since he wasn't needed at that moment, but the office wouldn't be open until ten, as the recording informed him. The recording was a very pretty girl with red hair, tourmaline eyes, and a very sexy voice. Tom would have been more impressed if he had not known her. She had played in some small parts in two of his shows, and the maddening voice was not hers. Neither was the color of her eyes.

At noon he called again, got through after a ten-minute wait, and asked Mrs. Bellefield if she would put through a request for him. Mrs. Bellefield reprimanded him for not having phoned sooner; she was not sure that anything could be done today. He tried to tell her his circumstances and then gave up. Bureaucrats! That evening he went to a public emergency place, slept for the required four hours while the inductive field speeded up his dreaming, woke up, and got into the upright cylinder of eternium. He stood for ten seconds, gazing out through the transparent door at other cylinders with their still figures, and then he pressed the button. Approximately fifteen seconds later he became unconscious.

He had to spend three more nights in the public stoner. Three days of fall were gone; only five left. Not that that mattered in California so much. When he had lived in Chicago, winter was like a white blanket being shaken by a madwoman. Spring was a green explosion. Summer was a bright roar and a hot breath. Fall was the topple of a drunken jester in garish motley.

The fourth day, he received notice that he could move into the very house he had picked. This surprised and pleased him. He knew of a dozen who had spent a whole year—forty-eight days or so—in a public station while waiting. He moved in the fifth day with three days of spring to enjoy. But he would have to use up his two days off to shop for clothes, bring in groceries and other goods, and get acquainted with his housemates. Sometimes, he wished he had not been born with the compulsion to act, TV'ers worked five days at a stretch, sometimes six, while a plumber, for instance, only put in three days out of seven.

The house was as large as the other, and the six extra blocks to walk would be good for him. It held eight people per day, counting himself. He moved in that evening, introduced himself, and got Mabel Curta, who worked as a secretary for a producer, to fill him in on the household routine. After he made sure that his stoner had been moved into the stoner room, he could relax somewhat.

Mabel Curta had accompanied him into the stoner room, since she had appointed herself his guide. She was a short, overly curved woman of about thirty-five (Tuesday time). She had been divorced three times, and marriage was no more for her unless, of course, Mr. Right came along. Tom was between marriages himself, but he did not tell her so.

"We'll take a look at your bedroom," Mabel said. "It's small but it's soundproofed, thank God."

He started after her, then stopped. She looked back through the doorway and said, "What is it?"

"This girl..."

There were sixty-three of the tall gray eternium cylinders. He was looking through the door of the nearest at the girl within.

"Wow! Really beautiful!"

If Mabel felt any jealousy, she suppressed it.

"Yes, isn't she!"

The girl had long, black, slightly curly hair, a face that could have launched him a thousand times a thousand times, a figure that had enough but not too much, and long legs. Her eyes were open; in the dim light they looked a purplish-blue. She wore a thin silvery dress.

The plate by the top of the door gave her vital data. Jennie Marlowe. Born 2031 A.D., San Marino, California. She would be twenty-four years old. Actress. Unmarried. Wednesday's child.

"What's the matter?" Mabel said.

"Nothing."

How could he tell her that he felt sick in his stomach from a desire that could never be satisfied? Sick from beauty?

> For will in us is over-ruled by fate.
> Who ever loved, that loved not at first sight?

"What?" Mabel said, and then, after laughing, "You must be kidding?"

She wasn't angry. She realized that Jennie Marlowe was no more competition than if she were dead. She was right. Better for him to busy himself with the living of this world. Mabel wasn't too bad, cuddly, really, and, after a few drinks, rather stimulating.

They went downstairs afterward after 18:00 to the TV room. Most of the others were there, too. Some had their ear plugs in;

some were looking at the screen but talking. The newscast was on, of course. Everybody was filling up on what had happened last Tuesday and today. The Speaker of the House was retiring after his term was up. His days of usefulness were over and his recent ill health showed no signs of disappearing. There was a shot of the family graveyard in Mississippi with the pedestal reserved for him. When science someday learned how to rejuvenate, he would come out of stonerment.

"That'll be the day!" Mabel said. She squirmed on his lap.

"Oh, I think they'll crack it," he said. "They're already on the track; they've succeeded in stopping the aging of rabbits."

"I don't mean that," she said. "Sure, they'll find out how to rejuvenate people. But then what? You think they're going to bring them all back? With all the people they got now and then they'll double, maybe triple, maybe quadruple, the population? You think they won't just leave them standing there?" She giggled, and said, "What would the pigeons do without them?"

He squeezed her waist. At the same time, he had a vision of himself squeezing *that* girl's waist. Hers would be soft enough but with no hint of fat.

Forget about her. Think of now. Watch the news.

A Mrs. Wilder had stabbed her husband and then herself with a kitchen knife. Both had been stonered immediately after the police arrived, and they had been taken to the hospital. An investigation of a work slowdown in the county government offices was taking place. The complaints were that Monday's people were not setting up the computers for Tuesday's. The case was being referred to the proper authorities of both days. The Ganymede base reported that the Great Red Spot of Jupiter was emitting weak but definite pulses that did not seem to be random.

The last five minutes of the program was a precis devoted to outstanding events of the other days. Mrs. Cuthmar, the housemother, turned the channel to a situation comedy with no protests from anybody.

Tom left the room, after telling Mabel that he was going to bed early—alone, and to sleep. He had a hard day tomorrow.

He tiptoed down the hall and the stairs and into the stoner room. The lights were soft, there were many shadows, and it was quiet. The sixty-three cylinders were like ancient granite

54

columns of an underground chamber of a buried city. Fifty-five faces were white blurs behind the clear metal. Some had their eyes open; most had closed them while waiting for the field radiated from the machine in the base. He looked through Jennie Marlowe's door. He felt sick again. Out of his reach; never for him. Wednesday was only a day away. No, it was only a little less than four and a half hours away.

He touched the door. It was slick and only a little cold. She stared at him. Her right forearm was bent to hold the strap of a large purse. When the door opened, she would step out, ready to go. Some people took their showers and fixed their faces as soon as they got up from their sleep and then went directly into the stoner. When the field was automatically radiated at 05:00, they stepped out a minute later, ready for the day.

He would like to step out of his "coffin," too, at the same time.

But he was barred by Wednesday.

He turned away. He was acting like a sixteen-year-old kid. He had been sixteen about one hundred and six years ago, not that that made any difference. Physiologically, he was thirty.

As he started up to the second floor, he almost turned around and went back for another look. But he took himself by his neck-collar and pulled himself up to his room. There he decided he would get to sleep at once. Perhaps he would dream about her. If dreams were wish-fulfillments, they would bring her to him. It still had not been "proved" that dreams always expressed wishes, but it had been proved that man deprived of dreaming did go mad. And so the somniums radiated a field that put man into a state in which he got all the sleep, and all the dreams, that he needed within a four-hour period. Then he was awakened and a little later went into the stoner where the field suspended all atomic and subatomic activity. He would remain in that state forever unless the activating field came on.

He slept, and Jennie Marlowe did not come to him. Or, if she did, he did not remember. He awoke, washed his face, went down eagerly to the stoner, where he found the entire household standing around, getting in one last smoke, talking, laughing. Then they would step into their cylinders, and a silence like that at the heart of a mountain would fall.

He had often wondered what would happen if he did not go

into the stoner. How would he feel? Would he be panicked? All his life, he had known only Tuesdays. Would Wednesday rush at him, roaring, like a tidal wave? Pick him up and hurl him against the reefs of a strange time?

What if he made some excuse and went back upstairs and did not go back down until the field had come on? By then, he could not enter. The door to his cylinder would not open again until the proper time. He could still run down to the public emergency stoners only three blocks away. But if he stayed in his room, waiting for Wednesday?

Such things happened. If the breaker of the law did not have a reasonable excuse, he was put on trial. It was a felony second only to murder to "break time," and the unexcused were stonered. All felons, sane or insane, were stonered. Or *mañanaed*, as some said. The *mañanaed* criminal waited in immobility and unconsciousness, preserved unharmed until science had techniques to cure the insane, the neurotic, the criminal, the sick. *Mañana.*

"What was it like in Wednesday?" Tom had asked a man who had been unavoidably left behind because of an accident.

"How would I know? I was knocked out except for about fifteen minutes. I was in the same city, and I had never seen the faces of the ambulance men, of course, but then I've never seen them here. They stonered me and left me in the hospital for Tuesday to take care of."

He must have it bad, he thought. Bad. Even to think of such a thing was crazy. Getting into Wednesday was almost impossible. Almost. But it could be done. It would take time and patience, but it could be done.

He stood in front of his stoner for a moment. The others said, "See you! So long! Next Tuesday!" Mabel called, "Good night, lover!"

"Good night," he muttered.

"What?" she shouted.

"Good night!"

He glanced at the beautiful face behind the door. Then he smiled. He had been afraid that she might hear him say good night to a woman who called him lover.

He had ten minutes left. The intercom alarms were whooping. Get going, everybody! Time to take the six-day trip! Run! Remember the penalties!

He remembered, but he wanted to leave a message. The recorder was on a table. He activated it, and said, "Dear *Miss* Jennie Marlowe. My name is Tom Pym, and my stoner is next to yours. I am an actor, too; in fact, I work at the same studio as you. I know this is presumptuous of me, but I have never seen anybody so beautiful. Do you have a talent to match your beauty? I would like to see some run-offs of your shows. Would you please leave some in room five? I'm sure the occupant won't mind. Yours, Tom Pym."

He ran it back. It was certainly bald enough, and that might be just what was needed. Too flowery or too pressing would have made her leery. He had commented on her beauty twice but not overstressed it. And the appeal to her pride in her acting would be difficult to resist. Nobody knew better than he about that.

He whistled a little on his way to the cylinder. Inside, he pressed the button and looked at his watch. Five minutes to midnight. The light on the huge screen above the computer in the police station would not be flashing for him. Ten minutes from now, Wednesday's police would step out of their stoners in the precinct station, and they would take over their duties.

There was a ten-minute hiatus between the two days in the police station. All hell could break loose in these few minutes and it sometimes did. But a price had to be paid to maintain the walls of time.

He opened his eyes. His knees sagged a little and his head bent. The activation was a million microseconds fast—from eternium to flesh and blood almost instantaneously and the heart never knew that it had been stopped for such a long time. Even so, there was a little delay in the muscles' response to a standing position.

He pressed the button, opened the door, and it was as if his button had launched the day. Mabel had made herself up last night so that she looked dawn-fresh. He complimented her and she smiled happily. But he told her he would meet her for breakfast. Halfway up the staircase, he stopped, and waited until the hall was empty. Then he sneaked back down and into the stoner room. He turned on the recorder.

A voice, husky but also melodious, said, "Dear Mister Pym. I've had a few messages from other days. It was fun to talk back and forth across the abyss between the worlds, if you don't mind my exaggerating a little. But there is really no sense in it, once the novelty has worn off. If you become interested in the other person, you're frustrating yourself. That person can only be a voice in a recorder and a cold waxy face in a metal coffin. I wax poetic. Pardon me. If the person doesn't interest you, why continue to communicate? There is no sense in either case. And I *may* be beautiful. Anyway, I thank you for the compliment, but I am also sensible.

"I should have just not bothered to reply. But I want to be nice; I didn't want to hurt your feelings. So please don't leave any more messages."

He waited while silence was played. Maybe she was pausing for effect. Now would come a chuckle or a low honey-throated laugh, and she would say, "However, I don't like to disappoint my public. The run-offs are in your room."

The silence stretched out. He turned off the machine and went to the dining room for breakfast.

Siesta time at work was from 14:40 to 14:45. He lay down on the bunk and pressed the button. Within a minute he was asleep. He did dream of Jennie this time; she was a white shimmering figure solidifying out of the darkness and floating toward him. She was even more beautiful than she had been in her stoner.

The shooting ran overtime that afternoon so that he got home just in time for supper. Even the studio would not dare keep a man past his supper hour, especially since the studio was authorized to serve food only at noon.

He had time to look at Jennie for a minute before Mrs. Cuthmar's voice screeched over the intercom. As he walked down the hall, he thought, "I'm getting barnacled on her. It's ridiculous. I'm a grown man. Maybe . . . maybe I should see a psycher."

Sure, make your petition, and wait until a psycher has time for you. Say about three hundred days from now, if you are lucky. And if the psycher doesn't work out for you, then petition for another, and wait six hundred days.

Petition. He slowed down. Petition. What about a request, not to see a psycher, but to move? Why not? What did he have to lose? It would probably be turned down, but he could at least try.

Even obtaining a form for the request was not easy. He spent two nonwork days standing in line at the Center City Bureau before he got the proper forms. The first time, he was handed the wrong form and had to start all over again. There was no line set aside for those who wanted to change their days. There were not enough who wished to do this to justify such a line. So he had to queue up before the Miscellaneous office counter of the Mobility Section of the Vital Exchange Department of the Interchange and Cross Transfer Bureau. None of these titles had anything to do with emigration to another day.

When he got his form the second time, he refused to move from the office window until he had checked the number of the form and asked the clerk to double-check. He ignored the cries and the mutterings behind him. Then he went to one side of the vast room and stood in line before the punch machines. After two hours, he got to sit down at a small rolltop desk-shaped machine, above which was a large screen. He inserted the form into the slot, looked at the projection of the form, and punched buttons to mark the proper spaces opposite the proper questions. After that, all he had to do was to drop the form into a slot and hope it did not get lost. Or hope he would not have to go through the same procedure because he had improperly punched the form.

That evening, he put his head against the hard metal and murmured to the rigid face behind the door, "I must really love you to go through all this. And you don't even know it. And, worse, if you did, you might not care one bit."

To prove to himself that he had kept his gray stuff, he went out with Mabel that evening to a party given by Sol Voremwolf, a producer. Voremwolf had just passed a civil service examination giving him an A-13 rating. This meant that, in time, with some luck and the proper pull, he would become an executive vice-president of the studio.

The party was a qualified success. Tom and Mabel returned about half an hour before stoner time. Tom had managed to refrain from too many blowminds and liquor, so he was not tempted by Mabel. Even so, he knew that when he became unstonered, he would be half-loaded and he'd have to take some dreadful counter-actives. He would look and feel like hell at work, since he had missed his sleep.

He put Mabel off with an excuse, and went down to the

stoner room ahead of the others. Not that that would do him any good if he wanted to get stonered early. The stoners only activated within narrow time limits.

He leaned against the cylinder and patted the door. "I tried not to think about you all evening. I wanted to be fair to Mabel, it's not fair to go out with her and think about you all the time."

All's fair in love...

He left another message for her, then wiped it out. What was the use? Besides, he knew that his speech was a little thick. He wanted to appear at his best for her.

Why should he? What did she care for him?

The answer was, he did care, and there was no reason or logic connected with it. He loved this forbidden, untouchable, far-away-in-time, yet-so-near woman.

Mabel had come in silently. She said, "You're sick!"

Tom jumped away. Now why had he done that? He had nothing to be ashamed of. Then why was he so angry with her? His embarrassment was understandable but his anger was not.

Mabel laughed at him, and he was glad. Now he could snarl at her. He did so, and she turned away and walked out. But she was back in a few minutes with the others. It would soon be midnight.

By then he was standing inside the cylinder. A few seconds later, he left it, pushed Jennie's backward on its wheels, and pushed his around so that it faced hers. He went back in, pressed the button, and stood there. The double doors only slightly distorted his view. But she seemed even more removed in distance, in time, and in unattainability.

Three days later, well into winter, he received a letter. The box inside the entrance hall buzzed just as he entered the front door. He went back and waited until the letter was printed and had dropped out from the slot. It was the reply to his request to move to Wednesday.

Denied. Reason: he had no reasonable reason to move.

That was true. But he could not give his real motive. It would have been even less impressive than the one he had given. He had punched the box opposite No. 12. REASON: TO GET INTO AN ENVIRONMENT WHERE MY TALENTS WILL BE

MORE LIKELY TO BE ENCOURAGED.

He cursed and he raged. It was his human, his civil right to move into any day he pleased. That is, it should be his right. What if a move did cause much effort? What if it required a transfer of his I.D. and all the records connected with him from the moment of his birth? What if...?

He could rage all he wanted to, but it would not change a thing. He was stuck in the world of Tuesday.

Not yet, he muttered. Not yet. Fortunately, there is no limit to the number of requests I can make in my own day. I'll send out another. They think they can wear me out, huh? Well, I'll wear them out. Man against the machine. Man against the system. Man against the bureaucracy and the hard cold rules.

Winter's twenty days had sped by. Spring's eight days rocketed by. It was summer again. On the second day of the twelve days of summer, he received a reply to his second request.

It was neither a denial nor an acceptance. It stated that if he thought he would be better off psychologically in Wednesday because his astrologer said so, then he would have to get a psycher's critique of the astrologer's analysis. Tom Pym jumped into the air and clicked his sandaled heels together. Thank God that he lived in an age that did not classify astrologers as charlatans! The people—the masses—had protested that astrology was a necessity and that it should be legalized and honored. So laws were passed, and because of that, Tom Pym had a chance.

He went down to the stoner room and kissed the door of the cylinder and told Jennie Marlowe the good news. She did not respond, though he thought he saw her eyes brighten just a little. That was, of course, only his imagination, but he liked his imagination.

Getting a psycher for a consultation and getting through the three sessions took another year, another forty-eight days. Doctor Sigmund Traurig was a friend of Doctor Stelhela, the astrologer, and so that made things easier for Tom.

"I've studied Doctor Stelhela's chart carefully and analyzed carefully your obsession for this woman," he said. "I agree with Doctor Stelhela that you will always be unhappy in Tuesday, but I don't quite agree with him that you will be happier in Wednesday. However, you have this thing going for this Miss

Marlowe, so I think you should go to Wednesday. But only if you sign papers agreeing to see a psycher there for extended therapy."

Only later did Tom Pym realize that Doctor Traurig might have wanted to get rid of him because he had too many patients. But that was an uncharitable thought.

He had to wait while the proper papers were transmitted to Wednesday's authorities. His battle was only half-won. The other officials could turn him down. And if he did get to his goal, then what? She could reject him without giving him a second chance.

It was unthinkable, but she could.

He caressed the door and then pressed his lips against it.

"Pygmalion could at least touch Galatea," he said. "Surely, the gods—the big dumb bureaucrats—will take pity on me, who can't even touch you. Surely."

The psycher had said that he was incapable of a true and lasting bond with a woman, as so many men were in this world of easy-come-easy-go liaisons. He had fallen in love with Jennie Marlowe for several reasons. She may have resembled somebody he had loved when he was very young. His mother, perhaps? No? Well, never mind. He would find out in Wednesday— perhaps. The deep, the important, truth was that he loved Miss Marlowe because she could never reject him, kick him out, or become tiresome, complain, weep, yell, insult, and so forth. He loved her because she was unattainable and silent.

"I love her as Achilles must have loved Helen when he saw her on top of the walls of Troy," Tom said.

"I wasn't aware that Achilles was ever in love with Helen of Troy," Doctor Traurig said drily.

"Homer never said so, but I *know* that he must have been! Who could see her and *not* love her?"

"How the hell would I know? I never saw her! If I had suspected these delusions would intensify..."

"I am a poet!" Tom said.

"Overimaginative, you mean! Hmmm. She must be a douser! I don't have anything particular to do this evening. I'll tell you what...my curiosity is aroused...I'll come down to your place tonight and take a look at this fabulous beauty, your Helen of Troy."

Doctor Traurig appeared immediately after supper, and Tom Pym ushered him down the hall and into the stoner room at the rear of the big house as if he were a guide conducting a famous critic to a just-discovered Rembrandt.

The doctor stood for a long time in front of the cylinder. He hmmmed several times and checked her vital-data plate several times. Then he turned and said, "I see what you mean, Mr. Pym. Very well. I'll give the go-ahead."

"Ain't she something?" Tom said on the porch. "She's out of this world, literally and figuratively, of course."

"Very beautiful. But I believe that you are facing a great disappointment, perhaps heartbreak, perhaps, who knows, even madness, much as I hate to use that unscientific term."

"I'll take the chance," Tom said. "I know I sound nuts, but where would we be if it weren't for nuts? Look at the man who invented the wheel, at Columbus, at James Watt, at the Wright brothers, at Pasteur, you name them."

"You can scarcely compare these pioneers of science with their passion for truth with you and your desire to marry a woman. But, as I have observed, she is strikingly beautiful. Still, that makes me exceedingly cautious. Why isn't she married? What's wrong with her?"

"For all I know, she may have been married a dozen times!" Tom said. "The point is, she isn't now! Maybe she's disappointed and she's sworn to wait until the right man comes along. Maybe..."

"There's no maybe about it, you're neurotic," Traurig said. "But I actually believe that it would be more dangerous for you *not* to go to Wednesday than it would be *to* go."

"Then you'll say yes!" Tom said, grabbing the doctor's hand and shaking it.

"Perhaps. I have some doubts."

The doctor had a faraway look. Tom laughed and released the hand and slapped the doctor on the shoulder. "Admit it! You were really struck by her! You'd have to be dead not to!"

"She's all right," the doctor said. "But you must think this over. If you do go there and she turns you down, you might go off the deep end, much as I hate to use such a poetical term."

"No, I won't. I wouldn't be a bit the worse off. Better off, in fact. I'll at least get to see her in the flesh."

Spring and summer zipped by. Then, a morning he would never forget, the letter of acceptance. With it, instructions on how to get to Wednesday. These were simple enough. He was to make sure that the technicians came to his stoner sometime during the day and readjusted the timer within the base. He could not figure out why he could not just stay out of the stoner and let Wednesday catch up to him, but by now he was past trying to fathom the bureaucratic mind.

He did not intend to tell anyone at the house, mainly because of Mabel. But Mabel found out from someone at the studio. She wept when she saw him at supper time, and she ran upstairs to her room. He felt badly, but he did not follow to console her.

That evening, his heart beating hard, he opened the door to his stoner. The others had found out by then; he had been unable to keep the business to himself. Actually, he was glad that he had told them. They seemed happy for him, and they brought in drinks and had many rounds of toasts. Finally, Mabel came downstairs, wiping her eyes, and she said she wished him luck, too. She had known that he was not really in love with her. But she did wish someone would fall in love with her just by looking inside her stoner.

When she found out that he had gone to see Doctor Traurig, she said, "He's a very influential man. Sol Voremwolf had him for his analyst. He says he's even got influence on other days. He edits the *Psyche Crosscurrents*, you know, one of the few periodicals read by other people."

Other, of course, meant those who lived in Wednesdays through Mondays.

Tom said he was glad he had gotten Traurig. Perhaps he had used his influence to get the Wednesday authorities to push through his request so swiftly. The walls between the worlds were seldom broken, but it was suspected that the very influential did it when they pleased.

Now, quivering, he stood before Jennie's cylinder again. The last time, he thought, that I'll see her stonered. Next time, she'll be warm, colorful, touchable flesh.

"Ave atque vale!" he said aloud. The others cheered. Mabel said, "How corny!" They thought he was addressing them, and perhaps he had included them.

He stepped inside the cylinder, closed the door, and pressed the button. He would keep his eyes open, so that . . .

And today was Wednesday. Though the view was exactly the same, it was like being on Mars.

He pushed open the door and stepped out. The seven people had faces he knew and names he had read on their plates. But he did not know them.

He started to say hello, and then he stopped.

Jennie Marlowe's cylinder was gone.

He seized the nearest man by the arm.

"Where's Jennie Marlowe?"

"Let go. You're hurting me. She's gone. To Tuesday."

"Tuesday! Tuesday?"

"Sure. She'd been trying to get out of here for a long time. She had something about this day being unlucky for her. She was unhappy, that's for sure. Just two days ago, she said her application had finally been accepted. Apparently, some Tuesday psycher had used his influence. He came down and saw her in her stoner and that was it, brother."

The walls and the people and the stoners seemed to be distorted. Time was bending itself this way and that. He wasn't in Wednesday; he wasn't in Tuesday. He wasn't in *any* day. He was stuck inside himself at some crazy date that should never have existed.

"She can't do that!"

"Oh, no! She just did that!"

"But . . . you can't transfer more than once!"

"That's her problem."

It was his, too.

"I should never have brought him down to look at her!" Tom said. "The swine! The unethical swine!"

Tom Pym stood there for a long time, and then he went into the kitchen. It was the same environment, if you discounted the people. Later, he went to the studio and got a part in a situation play which was, really, just like all those in Tuesday. He watched the newscaster that night. The President of the U.S.A. had a different name and face, but the words of his speech could have been those of Tuesday's President. He was introduced to a secretary of a producer; her name wasn't Mabel, but it might as well have been.

The difference here was that Jennie was gone, and oh, what a world of difference it made to him.

THE FUNERAL

Kate Wilhelm

This cool, quiet frightening story was one of the ornaments of
Harlan Ellison's enormous anthology, *Again, Dangerous
Visions,* and a dangerous vision indeed it is, like all of Kate
Wilhelm's work. Her visions are dangerous because her vision is
unobstructed: she sees clearly, and what she sees is the truth, and
she puts it to paper. In an age that took its writers more seriously
than we do, she would have been burned at the stake.

No one could say exactly how old Madam Westfall was when
she finally died. At least one hundred twenty, it was estimated.
At the very least. For twenty years Madam Westfall had been a
shell containing the very latest products of advances made in
gerontology, and now she was dead. What lay on the viewing
dais was merely a painted, funereally garbed husk.

"She isn't real," Carla said to herself. "It's a doll, or something. It isn't really Madam Westfall." She kept her head bowed, and didn't move her lips, but she said the words over and over. She was afraid to look at a dead person. *The second time they slaughtered all those who bore arms, unguided, mindless now, but lethal with the arms caches that they used indiscriminately.*

Carla felt goose bumps along her arms and legs. She wondered if anyone else had been hearing the old Teacher's words.

The line moved slowly, all the girls in their long grey skirts had their heads bowed, their hands clasped. The only sound down the corridor was the sush-sush of slippers on plastic flooring, the occasional rustle of a skirt.

The viewing room had a pale green plastic floor, frosted-green plastic walls, and floor-to-ceiling windows that were now slits of brilliant light from a westering sun. All the furniture had been taken from the room, all the ornamentation. There were no flowers, nothing but the dais, and the bedlike box covered by a transparent shield. And the Teachers. Two at the dais, others between the light strips, at the doors. Their white hands clasped against black garb, heads bowed, hair slicked against each head, straight parts emphasizing bilateral symmetry. The Teachers didn't move, didn't look at the dais, at the girls parading past it.

Carla kept her head bowed, her chin tucked almost inside the V of her collarbone. The serpentine line moved steadily, very slowly. "She isn't real," Carla said to herself, desperately now.

She crossed the line that was the cue to raise her head; it felt too heavy to lift, her neck seemed paralyzed. When she did move, she heard a joint crack, and although her jaws suddenly ached, she couldn't relax.

The second green line. She turned her eyes to the right and looked at the incredibly shrunken, hardly human mummy. She felt her stomach lurch and for a moment she thought she was going to vomit. "She isn't real. It's a doll. She isn't real!" The third line. She bowed her head, pressed her chin hard against her collarbone, making it hurt. She couldn't swallow now, could hardly breathe. The line proceeded to the South Door and through it into the corridor.

She turned left at the South Door and, with her eyes downcast, started the walk back to her genetics class. She looked

neither right nor left, but she could hear others moving in the
same direction, slippers on plastic, the swish of a skirt, and when
she passed by the door to the garden she heard laughter of some
Ladies who had come to observe the viewing. She slowed down.

She felt the late sun hot on her skin at the open door and with
a sideways glance, not moving her head, she looked quickly into
the glaring greenery, but could not see them. Their laughter
sounded like music as she went past the opening.

"That one, the one with the blue eyes and straw-colored hair.
Stand up, girl."

Carla didn't move, didn't realize she was being addressed
until a Teacher pulled her from her seat.

"Don't hurt her! Turn around, girl. Raise your skirts, higher.
Look at me, child. Look up, let me see your face..."

"She's too young for choosing," said the Teacher, examining
Carla's bracelet. "Another year, Lady."

"A pity. She'll coarsen in a year's time. The fuzz is so soft
right now, the flesh so tender. Oh, well...." She moved away,
flicking a red skirt about her thighs, her red-clad legs narrowing
to tiny ankles, flashing silver slippers with heels that were like
icicles. She smelled... Carla didn't know any words to describe
how she smelled. She drank in the fragrance hungrily.

"Look at me, child. Look up, let me see your face...." The
words sang through her mind over and over. At night, falling
asleep, she thought of the face, drawing it up from the deep
black, trying to hold it in focus: white skin, pink cheek ridges,
silver eyelids, black lashes longer than she had known lashes
could be, silver-pink lips, three silver spots—one at the corner of
her left eye, another at the corner of her mouth, the third like a
dimple in the satiny cheek. Silver hair that was loose, in waves
about her face, that rippled with life of its own when she moved.
If only she had been allowed to touch the hair, to run her finger
over that cheek... The dream that began with the music of the
Lady's laughter ended with the nightmare of her other words:
"She'll coarsen in a year's time...."

After that Carla had watched the changes take place on and
within her body, and she understood what the Lady had meant.
Her once smooth legs began to develop hair; it grew under her
arms, and, most shameful, it sprouted as a dark, coarse bush
under her belly. She wept. She tried to pull the hairs out, but it

hurt too much, and made her skin sore and raw. Then she started
to bleed, and she lay down and waited to die, and was happy that
she would die. Instead, she was ordered to the infirmary and was
forced to attend a lecture on feminine hygiene. She watched in
stony-faced silence while the Doctor added the new information
to her bracelet. The Doctor's face was smooth and pink, her
eyebrows pale, her lashes so colorless and stubby that they were
almost invisible. On her chin was a brown mole with two long
hairs. She wore a straight blue-grey gown that hung from her
shoulders to the floor. Her drab hair was pulled back tightly
from her face, fastened in a hard bun at the back of her neck.
Carla hated her. She hated the Teachers. Most of all she hated
herself. She yearned for maturity.

Madam Westfall had written: "Maturity brings grace,
beauty, wisdom, happiness. Immaturity means ugliness,
unfinished beings with potential only, wholly dependent upon
and subservient to the mature citizens."

There was a True-False quiz on the master screen in front of
the classroom. Carla took her place quickly and touch-typed her
ID number on the small screen of her machine.

She scanned the questions, and saw that they were all simple
declarative statements of truth. Her stylus ran down the True
column of her answer screen and it was done. She wondered why
they were killing time like this, what they were waiting for.
Madam Westfall's death had thrown everything off schedule.

Paperlike brown skin, wrinkled and hard, with lines crossing
lines, vertical, horizontal, diagonal, leaving little islands of flesh,
hardly   enough   to   coat   the   bones.   Cracked   voice,
incomprehensible: *they took away the music from the
air ... voices   from   the   skies ... erased   pictures   that
move ... boxes that sing and sob ...* Crazy talk. And, ... *only
one left that knows. Only one.*

Madam Trudeau entered the classroom and Carla understood why the class had been personalized that period. The
Teacher had been waiting for Madam Trudeau's appearance.
The girls rose hurriedly. Madam Trudeau motioned for them to
be seated once more.

"The following girls attended Madam Westfall during the
past five years." She read a list. Carla's name was included on
her list. On finishing it, she asked, "Is there anyone who attended

Madam Westfall whose name I did not read?"

There was a rustle from behind Carla. She kept her gaze fastened on Madam Trudeau. "Name?" the Teacher asked.

"Luella, Madam."

"You attended Madam Westfall? When?"

"Two years ago, Madam. I was a relief for Sonya, who became ill suddenly."

"Very well." Madam Trudeau added Luella's name to her list. "You will all report to my office at eight A.M. tomorrow morning. You will be excused from classes and duties at that time. Dismissed." With a bow she excused herself to the class Teacher and left the room.

Carla's legs twitched and ached. Her swim class was at eight each morning and she had missed it, had been sitting on the straight chair for almost two hours, when finally she was told to go into Madam Trudeau's office. None of the other waiting girls looked up when she rose and followed the attendant from the anteroom. Madam Trudeau was seated at an oversized desk that was completely bare, with a mirrorlike finish. Carla stood before it with her eyes downcast, and she could see Madam Trudeau's face reflected from the surface of the desk. Madam Trudeau was looking at a point over Carla's head, unaware that the girl was examining her features.

"You attended Madam Westfall altogether seven times during the past four years, is that correct?"

"I think it is, Madam."

"You aren't certain?"

"I . . . I don't remember, Madam."

"I see. Do you recall if Madam Westfall spoke to you during any of those times?"

"Yes, Madam."

"Carla, you are shaking. Are you frightened?"

"No, Madam."

"Look at me, Carla."

Carla's hands tightened, and she could feel her fingernails cutting into her hands. She thought of the pain, and stopped shaking. Madam Trudeau had pasty white skin, with peaked black eyebrows, sharp black eyes, black hair. Her mouth was wide and full, her nose long and narrow. As she studied the girl before her, it seemed to Carla that something changed in her expression, but she couldn't say what it was, or how it now differed from what it had been a moment earlier. A new intensity perhaps, a new interest.

"Carla, I've been looking over your records. Now that you are fourteen it is time to decide on your future. I shall propose your name for the Teachers' Academy on the completion of your current courses. As my protégée, you will quit the quarters you now occupy and attend me in my chambers. . . ." She narrowed her eyes. "What is the matter with you, girl? Are you ill?"

"No, Madam. I . . . I had hoped. I mean, I designated my choice last month. I thought . . ."

Madam Trudeau looked to the side of her desk where a records screen was lighted. She scanned the report, and her lips curled derisively. "A Lady. You would be a Lady!" Carla felt a blush fire her face, and suddenly her palms were wet with sweat. Madam Trudeau laughed, a sharp barking sound. She said, "The girls who attended Madam Westfall in life shall attend her in death. You will be on duty in the Viewing Room for two hours each day, and when the procession starts for the burial services in Scranton, you will be part of the entourage. Meanwhile, each day for an additional two hours immediately following your attendance in the Viewing Room you will meditate on the words of wisdom you have heard from Madam Westfall, and you will write down every word she ever spoke in your presence. For this purpose there will be placed a notebook and a pen in your cubicle, which you will use for no other reason. You will discuss this with no one except me. You, Carla, will prepare to move to my quarters immediately, where a learning cubicle will be awaiting you. Dismissed."

Her voice became sharper as she spoke, and when she finished the words were staccato. Carla bowed and turned to leave.

"Carla, you will find that there are certain rewards in being chosen as a Teacher."

Carla didn't know if she should turn and bow again, or stop where she was, or continue. When she hesitated, the voice came again, shorter, raspish. "Go. Return to your cubicle."

The first time, they slaughtered only the leaders, the rousers, . . . would be enough to defuse the bomb, leave the rest silent and powerless and malleable. . . .

71

Carla looked at the floor before her, trying to control the trembling in her legs. Madam Westfall hadn't moved, hadn't spoken. She was dead, gone. The only sound was the sush, sush of slippers. The green plastic floor was a glare that hurt her eyes. The air was heavy and smelled of death. Smelled the Lady, drank in the fragrance, longed to touch her. Pale, silvery-pink lips, soft, shiny, with two high peaks on the upper lip. The Lady stroked her face with fingers that were soft and cool and gentle.

...when their eyes become soft with unspeakable desires and their bodies show signs of womanhood, then let them have their duties chosen for them, some to bear the young for the society, some to become Teachers, some Nurses, Doctors, some to be taken as Lovers by the citizens, some to be...

Carla couldn't control the sudden start that turned her head to look at the mummy. The room seemed to waver, then steadied again. The tremor in her legs became stronger, harder to stop. She pressed her knees together hard, hurting them where bone dug into flesh and skin. Fingers plucking at the coverlet. Plucking bones, brown bones with horny nails.

Water. Girl, give me water. Pretty pretty. You would have been killed, you would have. Pretty. The last time they left no one over ten. No one at all. Ten to twenty-five.

Pretty. Carla said it to herself. Pretty. She visualized it as p-r-i-t-y. Pity with an r. Scanning the dictionary for p-r-i-t-y. Nothing. Pretty. *Afraid of shiny, pretty faces. Young, pretty faces.*

The trembling was all through Carla. Two hours. Eternity. She had stood here forever, would die here, unmoving, trembling, aching. A sigh and the sound of a body falling softly to the floor. Soft body crumbling so easily. Carla didn't turn her head. It must be Luella. So frightened of the mummy. She'd had nightmares every night since Madam Westfall's death. What made a body stay upright, when it fell so easily? Take it out, the thing that held it together, and down, down. Just to let go, to know what to take out and allow the body to fall like that into sleep. Teachers moved across her field of vision, two of them in their black gowns. Sush-sush. Returned with Luella, or someone, between them. No sound. Sush-sush.

The new learning cubicle was an exact duplicate of the old

one. Cot, learning machine, chair, partitioned-off commode and washbasin. And new, the notebook and pen. Carla never had had a notebook and pen before. There was the stylus that was attached to the learning machine, and the lighted square in which to write, that then vanished into the machine. She turned the blank pages of the notebook, felt the paper between her fingers, tore a tiny corner off one of the back pages, examined it closely, the jagged edge, the texture of the fragment; she tasted it. She studied the pen just as minutely; it had a pointed, smooth end, and it wrote black. She made a line, stopped to admire it, and crossed it with another line. She wrote very slowly, "Carla," started to put down her number, the one on her bracelet, then stopped in confusion. She never had considered it before, but she had no last name, none that she knew. She drew three heavy lines over the two digits she had put down.

At the end of the two hours of meditation she had written her name a number of times, had filled three pages with it, in fact, and had written one of the things that she could remember hearing from the grey lips of Madam Westfall: "Non-citizens are the property of the state."

The next day the citizens started to file past the dais. Carla breathed deeply, trying to sniff the fragrance of the passing Ladies, but they were too distant. She watched their feet, clad in shoes of rainbow colors: pointed toes, stiletto heels; rounded toes, carved heels; satin, sequined slippers.... And just before her duty ended for the day, the Males started to enter the room.

She heard a gasp, Luella again. She didn't faint this time, merely gasped once. Carla saw the feet and legs at the same time and she looked up to see a male citizen. He was very tall and thick, and was dressed in the blue-and-white clothing of a Doctor of Law. He moved into the sunlight and there was a glitter from gold at his wrists and his neck, and the gleam of a smooth polished head. He turned past the dais and his eyes met Carla's. She felt herself go lightheaded and hurriedly she ducked her head and clenched her hands. She thought he was standing still, looking at her, and she could feel her heart thumping hard. Her relief arrived then and she crossed the room as fast as she could without appearing indecorous.

Carla wrote: "Why did he scare me so much? Why have I

never seen a Male before? Why does everyone else wear colors while the girls and the Teachers wear black and grey?"

She drew a wavering line figure of a man, and stared at it, and then Xed it out. Then she looked at the sheet of paper with dismay. Now she had four ruined sheets of paper to dispose of.

Had she angered him by staring? Nervously she tapped on the paper and tried to remember what his face had been like. Had he been frowning? She couldn't remember. Why couldn't she think of anything to write for Madam Trudeau? She bit the end of the pen and then wrote slowly, very carefully: *"Society may dispose of its property as it chooses, following discussion with at least three members, and following permission which is not to be arbitrarily denied."*

Had Madam Westfall ever said that? She didn't know, but she had to write something, and that was the sort of thing that Madam Westfall had quoted at great length. She threw herself down on the cot and stared at the ceiling. For three days she had kept hearing the Madam's dead voice, but now when she needed to hear her again, nothing.

Sitting in the straight chair, alert for any change in the position of the ancient one, watchful, afraid of the old Teacher. Cramped, tired and sleepy. Half listening to mutterings, murmurings of exhaled and inhaled breaths that sounded like words that made no sense. . . . *Mama said hide child, hide don't move and Stevie wanted a razor for his birthday and Mama said you're too young, you're only nine and he said no Mama I'm thirteen don't you remember and Mama said hide child hide don't move at all and they came in hating pretty faces. . . .*

Carla sat up and picked up the pen again, then stopped. When she heard the words, they were so clear in her head, but as soon as they ended, they faded away. She wrote: "hating pretty faces . . . hide child . . . only nine." She stared at the words and drew a line through them.

Pretty faces. Madam Westfall had called her pretty, pretty.

The chimes for social hour were repeated three times and finally Carla opened the door of her cubicle and took a step into the anteroom, where the other protégées already had gathered. There were five. Carla didn't know any of them, but she had seen all of them from time to time in and around the school grounds.

Madam Trudeau was sitting on a high-backed chair that was covered with black. She blended into it, so that only her hands and her face seemed apart from the chair, dead-white hands and face. Carla bowed to her and stood uncertainly at her own door.

"Come in, Carla. It is social hour. Relax. This is Wanda, Louise, Stephanie, Mary, Dorothy." Each girl inclined her head slightly as her name was mentioned. Carla couldn't tell afterward which name went with which girl. Two of them wore the black-striped overskirt that meant they were in the Teachers' Academy. The other three still wore the grey of the lower school, as did Carla, with black bordering the hems.

"Carla doesn't want to be a Teacher," Madam Trudeau said dryly. "She prefers the paint box of a Lady." She smiled with her mouth only. One of the academy girls laughed. "Carla, you are not the first to envy the paint box and the bright clothes of the Ladies. I have something to show you. Wanda, the film."

The girl who had laughed touched a button on a small table, and on one of the walls a picture was projected. Carla caught her breath. It was a Lady, all gold and white, gold hair, gold eyelids, filmy white gown that ended just above her knees. She turned and smiled, holding out both hands, flashing jeweled fingers, long, gleaming nails that came to points. Then she reached up and took off her hair.

Carla felt that she would faint when the golden hair came off in the Lady's hands, leaving short, straight brown hair. She placed the gold hair on a ball, and then, one by one, stripped off the long gleaming nails, leaving her hands just hands, bony and ugly. The Lady peeled off her eyelashes and brows, and then patted a brown, thick coating of something on her face, and, with its removal, revealed pale skin with wrinkles about her eyes, with hard, deep lines beside her nose down to her mouth that had also changed, had become small and mean. Carla wanted to shut her eyes, turn away, and go back to her cubicle, but she didn't dare move. She could feel Madam Trudeau's stare, and the gaze seemed to burn.

The Lady took off the swirling gown, and under it was a garment Carla never had seen before that covered her from her breasts to her thighs. The stubby fingers worked at fasteners, and finally got the garment off, and there was her stomach, bigger, bulging, with cruel red lines where the garment had pinched and squeezed her. Her breasts drooped almost to her waist. Carla couldn't stop her eyes, couldn't make them not see, couldn't make herself not look at the rest of the repulsive body.

Madam Trudeau stood up and went to her door. "Show Carla the other two films." She looked at Carla then and said, "I order you to watch. I shall quiz you on the contents." She left the room.

The other two films showed the same Lady at work. First with a protégée, then with a male citizen. When they were over Carla stumbled back to her cubicle and vomited repeatedly until she was exhausted. She had nightmares that night.

How many days, she wondered, have I been here now? She no longer trembled, but became detached almost as soon as she took her place between two of the tall windows. She didn't try to catch a whiff of the fragrance of the Ladies, or try to get a glimpse of the Males. She had chosen one particular spot in the floor on which to concentrate, and she didn't shift her gaze from it.

They were old and full of hate, and they said, let us remake them in our image, and they did.

Madam Trudeau hated her, despised her. Old and full of hate...

"Why were you not chosen to become a Woman to bear young?"

"I am not fit, Madam. I am weak and timid."

"Look at your hips, thin, like a Males' hips. And your breasts, small and hard." Madam Trudeau turned away in disgust. "Why were you not chosen to become a Professional, a Doctor, or a Technician?"

"I am not intelligent enough, Madam. I require many hours of study to grasp the mathematics."

"So. Weak, frail, not too bright. Why do you weep?"

"I don't know, Madam. I am sorry."

"Go to your cubicle. You disgust me."

Staring at a flaw in the floor, a place where an indentation distorted the light, creating one very small oval shadow, wondering when the ordeal would end, wondering why she couldn't fill the notebook with the many things that Madam Westfall had said, things that she could remember here, and could not remember when she was in her cubicle with pen poised over the notebook.

Sometimes Carla forgot where she was, found herself in the chamber of Madam Westfall, watching the ancient one struggle to stay alive, forcing breaths in and out, refusing to admit death. Watching the incomprehensible dials and tubes and bottles of fluids with lowering levels, watching needles that vanished into flesh, tubes that disappeared under the bedclothes, that seemed to writhe now and again with a secret life, listening to the mumbling voice, the groans and sighs, the meaningless words.

Three times they rose against the children and three times slew them until there were none left none at all because the contagion had spread and all over ten were infected and carried radios. . . .

Radios? A disease? Infected with radios, spreading it among young people?

And Mama said hide child hide and don't move and put this in the cave too and don't touch it.

Carla's relief came and numbly she walked from the Viewing Room. She watched the movement of the black border of her skirt as she walked and it seemed that the blackness crept up her legs, enveloped her middle, climbed her front until it reached her neck, and then it strangled her. She clamped her jaws hard and continued to walk her measured pace.

The girls who had attended Madam Westfall in life were on duty throughout the school ceremonies after the viewing. They were required to stand in a line behind the dais. There were eulogies to the patience and firmness of the first Teacher. Eulogies to her wisdom in setting up the rules of the school. Carla tried to keep her attention on the speakers, but she was so tired and drowsy that she heard only snatches. Then she was jolted into awareness. Madam Trudeau was talking.

"... a book that will be the guide to all future Teachers, showing them the way through personal tribulations and trials to achieve the serenity that was Madam Westfall's. I am honored by this privilege, in choosing me and my apprentices to accomplish this end. . . ."

Carla thought of the gibberish that she had been putting down in her notebook and she blinked back tears of shame.

Madam Trudeau should have told them why she wanted the information. She would have to go back over it and destroy all the nonsense that she had written down.

Late that afternoon the entourage formed that would accompany Madam Westfall to her final ceremony in Scranton, her native city, where her burial would return her to her family.

Madam Trudeau had an interview with Carla before departure. "You will be in charge of the other girls," she said. "I expect you to maintain order. You will report any disturbance, or any infringement of rules, immediately, and if that is not possible, if I am occupied, you will personally impose order in my name."

"Yes, Madam."

"Very well. During the journey the girls will travel together in a compartment of the tube. Talking will be permitted, but no laughter, no childish play. When we arrive at the Scranton home, you will be given rooms with cots. Again you will all comport yourselves with the dignity of the office which you are ordered to fulfill at this time."

Carla felt excitement mount within her as the girls lined up to take their places along the sides of the casket. They went with it to a closed limousine, where they sat knee to knee, unspeaking, hot, to be taken over smooth highways for an hour to the tube. Madam Westfall had refused to fly in life, and was granted the same rights in death, so her body was to be transported from Wilmington to Scranton by the rocket tube. As soon as the girls had accompanied the casket to its car, and were directed to their own compartment, their voices raised in a babble. It was the first time any of them had left the school grounds since entering them at the age of five.

Ruthie was going to work in the infants' wards, and she turned faintly pink and soft-looking when she talked about it. Luella was a music apprentice already, having shown skill on the piano at an early age. Lorette preened herself slightly and announced that she had been chosen as a Lover by a gentleman. She would become a Lady one day. Carla stared at her curiously, wondering at her pleased look, wondering if she had not been shown the films yet. Lorette was blue-eyed, with pale hair, much the same build as Carla. Looking at her, Carla could imagine her in soft dresses, with her mouth painted, her hair covered by the other hair that was cloud-soft and shiny. . . . She looked at the girl's cheeks flushed with excitement at the thought of her future, and she knew that with or without the paint box, Lorette would be a Lady whose skin would be smooth, whose mouth would be soft. . . .

"The fuzz is so soft now, the flesh so tender." She remembered the scent, the softness of the Lady's hands, the way her skirt moved about her red-clad thighs.

She bit her lip. But she didn't want to be a Lady. She couldn't ever think of them again without loathing and disgust. She was chosen to be a Teacher.

They said it is the duty of society to prepare its non-citizens for citizenship but it is recognized that there are those who will not meet the requirements and society itself is not to be blamed for those occasional failures that must accrue.

She took out her notebook and wrote the words in it.

"Did you just remember something else she said?" Lisa asked. She was the youngest of the girls, only ten, and had attended Madam Westfall one time. She seemed to be very tired.

Carla looked over what she had written, and then read it aloud. "It's from the school rules book," she said. "Maybe changed a little, but the same meaning. You'll study it in a year or two."

Lisa nodded. "You know what she said to me? She said I should go hide in the cave, and never lose my birth certificate. She said I should never tell anyone where the radio is." She frowned. "Do you know what a cave is? And a radio?"

"You wrote it down, didn't you? In the notebook?"

Lisa ducked her head. "I forgot again. I remembered it once and then forgot again until now." She searched through her cloth travel bag for her notebook and when she didn't find it, she dumped the contents on the floor to search more carefully. The notebook was not there.

"Lisa, when did you have it last?"

"I don't know. A few days ago. I don't remember."

"When Madam Trudeau talked to you the last time, did you have it then?"

"No. I couldn't find it. She said if I didn't have it the next time I was called for an interview, she'd whip me. But I can't find it!" She broke into tears and threw herself down on her small heap of belongings. She beat her fists on them and sobbed. "She's going to whip me and I can't find it. I can't. It's gone."

Carla stared at her. She shook her head. "Lisa, stop that crying. You couldn't have lost it. Where? There's no place to lose it. You didn't take it from your cubicle, did you?"

The girl sobbed louder. "No. No. No. I don't know where it is."

Carla knelt by her and pulled the child up from the floor to a squatting position. "Lisa, what did you put in the notebook? Did you play with it?"

Lisa turned chalky white and her eyes became very large, then she closed them, no longer weeping.

"So you used it for other things? Is that it? What sort of things?"

Lisa shook her head. "I don't know. Just things."

"All of it? The whole notebook?"

"I couldn't help it. I didn't know what to write down. Madam Westfall said too much. I couldn't write it all. She wanted to touch me and I was afraid of her and I hid under the chair and she kept calling me, 'Child, come here, don't hide, I'm not one of them. Go to the cave and take it with you.' And she kept reaching for me with her hands. I . . . They were like chicken claws. She would have ripped me apart with them. She hated me. She said she hated me. She said I should have been killed with the others, why wasn't I killed with the others."

Carla, her hands hard on the child's shoulders, turned away from the fear and despair she saw on the girl's face.

Ruthie pushed past her and hugged the child. "Hush, hush, Lisa. Don't cry now. Hush. There, there."

Carla stood up and backed away. "Lisa, what sort of things did you put in the notebook?"

"Just things that I like. Snowflakes and flowers and designs."

"All right. Pick up your belongings and sit down. We must be nearly there. It seems like the tube is stopping."

Again they were shown from a closed compartment to a closed limousine and whisked over countryside that remained invisible to them. There was a drizzly rain falling when they stopped and got out of the car.

The Westfall house was a three-storied, pseudo-Victorian wooden building, with balconies and cupolas, and many chimneys. There was scaffolding about it, and one of the three porches had been torn away and was being replaced as restoration of the house, turning it into a national monument, progressed. The girls accompanied the casket to a gloomy, large room where the air was chilly and damp, and scant lighting cast deep shadows. After the casket had been positioned on the dais which also had accompanied it, the girls followed Madam Trudeau through narrow corridors, up narrow steps, to the third floor where two large rooms had been prepared for them, each containing seven cots.

Madam Trudeau showed them the bathroom that would serve their needs, told them goodnight, and motioned Carla to follow her. They descended the stairs to a second-floor room that had black, massive furniture: a desk, two straight chairs, a bureau with a wavery mirror over it, and a large canopied bed.

Madam Trudeau paced the black floor silently for several minutes without speaking, then she swung around and said, "Carla, I heard every word that silly little girl said this afternoon. She drew pictures in her notebook! This is the third time the word cave has come up in reports of Madam Westfall's mutterings. Did she speak to you of caves?"

Carla's mind was whirling. How had she heard what they had said? Did maturity also bestow magical abilities? She said, "Yes, Madam, she spoke of hiding in a cave."

"Where is the cave, Carla? Where is it?"

"I don't know, Madam. She didn't say."

Madam Trudeau started to pace once more. Her pale face was drawn in lines of concentration that carved deeply into her flesh, two furrows straight up from the inner brows, other lines at the sides of her nose, straight to her chin, her mouth tight and hard. Suddenly she sat down and leaned back in the chair. "Carla, in the last four or five years Madam Westfall became childishly senile; she was no longer living in the present most of the time, but was reliving incidents in her past. Do you understand what I mean?"

Carla nodded, then said hastily, "Yes, Madam."

"Yes. Well, it doesn't matter. You know that I have been commissioned to write the biography of Madam Westfall, to immortalize her writings and her utterances. But there is a gap, Carla. A large gap in our knowledge, and until recently it seemed that the gap never would be filled in. When Madam Westfall was found as a child, wandering in a dazed condition, undernourished, almost dead from exposure, she did not know who she was, where she was from, anything about her past at all. Someone had put an identification bracelet on her arm, a steel bracelet that she could not remove, and that was the only clue there was about her origins. For ten years she received the best medical care and education available, and her intellect sparkled brilliantly, but she never regained her memory."

Madam Trudeau shifted to look at Carla. A trick of the lighting made her eyes glitter like jewels. "You have studied how she started her first school with eight students, and over the next century developed her teaching methods to the point of perfection that we now employ throughout the nation, in the Males' school as well as the Females'. Through her efforts Teachers have become the most respected of all citizens and the schools the most powerful of all institutions." A mirthless smile crossed her face, gone almost as quickly as it formed, leaving the deep shadows, lines, and the glittering eyes. "I honored you more than you yet realize when I chose you for my protégée."

The air in the room was too close and dank, smelled of moldering wood and unopened places. Carla continued to watch Madam Trudeau, but she was feeling lightheaded and exhausted and the words seemed interminable to her. The glittering eyes held her gaze and she said nothing. The thought occurred to her that Madam Trudeau would take Madam Westfall's place as head of the school now.

"Encourage the girls to talk, Carla. Let them go on as much as they want about what Madam Westfall said, lead them into it if they stray from the point. Written reports have been sadly deficient." She stopped and looked questioningly at the girl. "Yes? What is it?"

"Then ... I mean after they talk, are they to write ...? Or should I try to remember and write it all down?"

"There will be no need for that," Madam Trudeau said. "Simply let them talk as much as they want."

"Yes, Madam."

"Very well. Here is a schedule for the coming days. Two girls on duty in the Viewing Room at all times from dawn until dark, yard exercise in the enclosed garden behind the building if the weather permits, kitchen duty, and so on. Study it, and direct the girls to their duties. On Saturday afternoon everyone will attend the burial, and on Sunday we return to the school. Now go."

Carla bowed, and turned to leave. Madam Trudeau's voice stopped her once more. "Wait, Carla. Come here. You may brush my hair before you leave."

Carla took the brush in numb fingers and walked obediently behind Madam Trudeau, who was loosening hair clasps that restrained her heavy black hair. It fell down her back like a dead snake, uncoiling slowly. Carla started to brush it.

"Harder, girl. Are you so weak that you can't brush hair?"

She plied the brush harder until her arm became heavy and then Madam Trudeau said, "Enough. You are a clumsy girl, awkward and stupid. Must I teach you everything, even how to brush one's hair properly?" She yanked the brush from Carla's hand and now there were two spots of color on her cheeks and her eyes were flashing. "Get out. Go! Leave me! On Saturday immediately following the funeral you will administer punishment to Lisa for scribbling in her notebook. Afterward report to me. And now get out of here!"

Carla snatched up the schedule and backed across the room, terrified of the Teacher who seemed demoniacal suddenly. She bumped into the other chair and nearly fell down. Madam Trudeau laughed shortly and cried, "Clumsy, awkward! You would be a Lady! You?"

Carla groped behind her for the doorknob and finally escaped into the hallway, where she leaned against the wall, trembling too hard to move on. Something crashed into the door behind her and she stifled a scream and ran. The brush. Madam had thrown the brush against the door.

Madam Westfall's ghost roamed all night, chasing shadows in and out of rooms, making the floors creak with her passage, echoes of her voice drifting in and out of the dorm where Carla tossed restlessly. Twice she sat upright in fear, listening intently, not knowing why. Once Lisa cried out and she went to her and held her hand until the child quieted again. When dawn lighted the room Carla was awake and standing at the windows looking at the ring of mountains that encircled the city. Black shadows against the lesser black of the sky, they darkened, and suddenly caught fire from the sun striking their tips. The fire spread downward, went out, and became merely light on the leaves that were turning red and gold. Carla turned from the view, unable to explain the pain that filled her. She awakened the first two girls who were to be on duty with Madam Westfall and after their quiet departure, returned to the window. The sun was all the way up now, but its morning light was soft; there were no hard outlines anywhere. The trees were a blend of colors with no individual boundaries, and rocks and earth melted together and were one. Birds were singing with the desperation of summer's end and winter's approach.

"Carla?" Lisa touched her arm and looked up at her with wide, fearful eyes. "Is she going to whip me?"

"You will be punished after the funeral," Carla said, stiffly. "And I should report you for touching me, you know."

The child drew back, looking down at the black border on Carla's skirt. "I forgot." She hung her head. "I'm...I'm so scared."

"It's time for breakfast, and after that we'll have a walk in the gardens. You'll feel better after you get out in the sunshine and fresh air."

"Chrysanthemums, dahlias, marigolds. No, the small ones there, with the brown fringes..." Luella pointed out the various flowers to the other girls. Carla walked in the rear, hardly listening, trying to keep her eye on Lisa, who also trailed behind. She was worried about the child. Lisa had not slept well, had eaten no breakfast, and was so pale and wan that she didn't look strong enough to take the short garden walk with them.

Eminent personages came and went in the gloomy old house and huddled together to speak in lowered voices. Carla paid little attention to them. "I can change it after I have some authority," she said to a still inner self who listened and made no reply. "What can I do now? I'm property. I belong to the state, to Madam Trudeau and the school. What good if I disobey and am also whipped? Would that help any? I won't hit her hard." The inner self said nothing, but she thought she could hear a mocking laugh come from the mummy that was being honored.

They had all those empty schools, miles and miles of school halls where no feet walked, desks where no students sat, books that no students scribbled up, and they put the children in them

84

and they could see immediately who couldn't keep up, couldn't learn the new ways, and they got rid of them. Smart. Smart of them. They were smart and had the goods and the money and the hatred. My God, they hated. That's who wins, who hates most. And is more afraid. Every time.

Carla forced her arms not to move, her hands to remain locked before her, forced her head to stay bowed. The voice now went on and on and she couldn't get away from it.

...rained every day cold freezing rain and Daddy didn't come back and Mama said, hide child, hide in the cave where it's warm, and don't move no matter what happens, don't move. Let me put it on your arm, don't take it off, never take it off show it to them if they find you show them make them look....

Her relief came and Carla left. In the wide hallway that led to the back steps she was stopped by a rough hand on her arm. "Damme, here's a likely one. Come here, girl. Let's have a look at you." She was spun around and the hand grasped her chin and lifted her head. "Did I say it! I could spot her all the way down the hall, now couldn't I? Can't hide what she's got with long skirts and that skinny hairdo, now can you? Didn't I spot her!" He laughed and turned Carla's head to the side and looked at her in profile, then laughed even louder.

She could see only that he was red-faced, with bushy eyebrows and thick grey hair. His hand holding her chin hurt, digging into her jaws at each side of her neck.

"Victor, turn her loose," the cool voice of a female said then. "She's been chosen already. An apprentice Teacher."

He pushed Carla from him, still holding her chin, and he looked down at the skirts with the broad black band at the bottom. He gave her a shove that sent her into the opposite wall. She clutched at it for support.

"Whose pet is she?" he said darkly.

"Trudeau's."

He turned and stamped away, not looking at Carla again. He wore the blue and white of a Doctor of Law. The female was a Lady in pink and black.

"Carla. Go upstairs." Madam Trudeau moved from an open doorway and stood before Carla. She looked up and down the shaking girl. "Now do you understand why I apprenticed you before this trip? For your own protection."

85

They walked to the cemetery on Saturday, a bright, warm day with golden light and the odor of burning leaves. Speeches were made, Madam Westfall's favorite music was played, and the services ended. Carla dreaded returning to the dormitory. She kept a close watch on Lisa, who seemed but a shadow of herself. Three times during the night she had held the girl until her nightmares subsided, and each time she had stroked her fine hair and soft cheeks and murmured to her quieting words, and she knew it was only her own cowardice that prevented her saying that it was she who would administer the whipping. The first shovelful of earth was thrown on top of the casket and everyone turned to leave the place, when suddenly the air was filled with raucous laughter, obscene chants, and wild music. It ended almost as quickly as it started, but the group was frozen until the mountain air became unnaturally still. Not even the birds were making a sound following the maniacal outburst.

Carla had been unable to stop the involuntary look that she cast about her at the woods that circled the cemetery. Who? Who would dare? Only a leaf or two stirred, floating downward on the gentle air effortlessly. Far in the distance a bird began to sing again, as if the evil spirits that had flown past were now gone.

"Madam Trudeau sent this up for you," Luella said nervously, handing Carla the rod. It was plastic, three feet long, thin, flexible. Carla looked at it and turned slowly to Lisa. The girl seemed to be swaying back and forth.

"I am to administer the whipping," Carla said. "You will undress now."

Lisa stared at her in disbelief, and then suddenly she ran across the room and threw herself on Carla, hugging her hard, sobbing. "Thank you, Carla. Thank you so much. I was so afraid, you don't know how afraid. Thank you. How did you make her let you do it? Will you be punished too? I love you so much, Carla." She was incoherent in her relief and she flung off her gown and underwear and turned around.

Her skin was pale and soft, rounded buttocks, dimpled just above the fullness. She had no waist yet, no breasts, no hair on her baby body. Like a baby she had whimpered in the night, clinging tightly to Carla, burying her head in the curve of Carla's breasts.

Carla raised the rod and brought it down, as easily as she could. Anything was too hard. There was a red welt. The girl bowed her head lower, but didn't whimper. She was holding the back of a chair and it jerked when the rod struck.

It would be worse if Madam Trudeau was doing it, Carla thought. She would try to hurt, would draw blood. Why? Why? The rod was hanging limply, and she knew it would be harder on both of them if she didn't finish it quickly. She raised it and again felt the rod bite into flesh, sending the vibration into her arm, through her body.

Again. The girl cried out, and a spot of blood appeared on her back. Carla stared at it in fascination and despair. She couldn't help it. Her arm wielded the rod too hard, and she couldn't help it. She closed her eyes a moment, raised the rod and struck again. Better. But the vibrations that had begun with the first flow increased, and she felt dizzy, and couldn't keep her eyes off the spot of blood that was trailing down the girl's back. Lisa was weeping now, her body was shaking. Carla felt a responsive tremor start within her.

Eight, nine. The excitement that stirred her was unnameable, unknowable, never before felt like this. Suddenly she thought of the Lady who had chosen her once, and scenes of the film she had been forced to watch flashed through her mind. . . . *remake them in our image.* She looked about in that moment frozen in time, and she saw the excitement on some of the faces, on others fear, disgust and revulsion. Her gaze stopped on Helga, who had her eyes closed, whose body was moving rhythmically. She raised the rod and brought it down as hard as she could, hitting the chair with a noise that brought everyone out of his own kind of trance. A sharp, cracking noise that was a finish.

"Ten!" she cried and threw the rod across the room.

Lisa turned and through brimming eyes, red, swollen, ugly with crying, said, "Thank you, Carla. It wasn't so bad."

Looking at her, Carla knew hatred. It burned through her, distorted the image of what she saw. Inside her body the excitement found no outlet, and it flushed her face, made her hands numb, and filled her with hatred. She turned and fled.

Before Madam Trudeau's door, she stopped a moment, took a deep breath, and knocked. After several moments the door opened and Madam Trudeau came out. Her eyes were glittering more than ever, and there were two spots of color on her pasty cheeks.

"It is done? Let me look at you." Her fingers were cold and moist when she lifted Carla's chin. "Yes, I see. I see. I am busy now. Come back in half an hour. You will tell me all about it. Half an hour." Carla never had seen a genuine smile on the Teacher's face before, and now when it came, it was more frightening than her frown was. Carla didn't move, but she felt as if every cell in her body had tried to pull back.

She bowed and turned to leave. Madam Trudeau followed her a step and said in a low vibrant voice, "You felt it, didn't you? You know now, don't you?"

"Madam Trudeau, are you coming back?" The door behind her opened, and one of the Doctors of Law appeared there.

"Yes, of course." She turned and went back to the room.

Carla let herself into the small enclosed area between the second and third floors, then stopped. She could hear the voices of girls coming down the stairs, going on duty in the kitchen, or outside for evening exercises. She stopped to wait for them to pass, and she leaned against the wall tiredly. This space was two and a half feet square perhaps. It was very dank and hot. From here she could hear every sound made by the girls on the stairs. Probably that was why the second door had been added, to muffle the noise of those going up and down. The girls had stopped on the steps and were discussing the laughter and obscenities they had heard in the cemetery.

Carla knew that it was her duty to confront them, to order them to their duties, to impose proper silence on them in public places, but she closed her eyes and pressed her hand hard on the wood behind her for support and wished they would finish their childish prattle and go on. The wood behind her started to slide.

She jerked away. A sliding door? She felt it and ran her finger along the smooth paneling to the edge where there was now a six-inch opening as high as she could reach and down to the floor. She pushed the door again and it slid easily, going between the two walls. When the opening was wide enough she stepped through it. The cave! She knew it was the cave that Madam

Westfall had talked about incessantly.

The space was no more than two feet wide, and very dark. She felt the inside door and there was a knob on it, low enough for children to reach. The door slid as smoothly from the inside as it had from the outside. She slid it almost closed and the voices were cut off, but she could hear other voices, from the room on the other side of the passage. They were not clear. She felt her way farther, and almost fell over a box. She held her breath as she realized that she was hearing Madam Trudeau's voice:

". . . be there. Too many independent reports of the old fool's babbling about it for there not to be something to it. Your men are incompetent."

"Trudeau, shut up. You scare the living hell out of the kids, but you don't scare me. Just shut up and accept the report. We've been over every inch of the hills for miles, and there's no cave. It was over a hundred years ago. Maybe there was one that the kids played in, but it's gone now. Probably collapsed."

"We have to be certain, absolutely certain."

"What's so important about it anyway? Maybe if you would give us more to go on we could make more progress."

"The reports state that when the militia came here, they found only Martha Westfall. They executed her on the spot without questioning her first. Fools! When they searched the house, they discovered that it was stripped. No jewels, no silver, diaries, papers. Nothing. Steve Westfall was dead. Dr. Westfall dead. Martha. No one has ever found the articles that were hidden, and when the child again appeared, she had true amnesia that never yielded to attempts to penetrate it."

"So, a few records, diaries. What are they to you?" There was silence, then he laughed. "The money! He took all his money out of the bank, didn't he?"

"Don't be ridiculous. I want records, that's all. There's a complete ham radio, complete. Dr. Westfall was an electronics engineer as well as a teacher. No one could begin to guess how much equipment he hid before he was killed."

Carla ran her hand over the box, felt behind it. More boxes.

"Yeah yeah. I read the reports, too. All the more reason to keep the search nearby. For a year before the end a close watch was kept on the house. They had to walk to wherever they hid the stuff. And I can just say again that there's no cave around here. It fell in."

"I hope so," Madam Trudeau said.

Someone knocked on the door, and Madam Trudeau called, "Come in."

"Yes, what is it? Speak up, girl."

"It is my duty to report, Madam, that Carla did not administer the full punishment ordered by you."

Carla's fists clenched hard. Helga.

"Explain," Madam Trudeau said sharply.

"She only struck Lisa nine times, Madam. The last time she hit the chair."

"I see. Return to your room."

The man laughed when the girl closed the door once more. "Carla is the golden one, Trudeau? The one who wears a single black band?"

"The one you manhandled earlier, yes."

"Insubordination in the ranks, Trudeau? Tut, tut. And your reports all state that you never have any rebellion. Never."

Very slowly Madam Trudeau said, "I have never had a student who didn't abandon any thoughts of rebellion under my guidance. Carla will be obedient. And one day she will be an excellent Teacher. I know the signs."

Carla stood before the Teacher with her head bowed and her hands clasped together. Madam Trudeau walked around her without touching her, then sat down and said, "You will whip Lisa every day for a week, beginning tomorrow."

Carla didn't reply.

"Don't stand mute before me, Carla. Signify your obedience immediately."

"I...I can't, Madam."

"Carla, any day that you do not whip Lisa, I will. And I will also whip you double her allotment. Do you understand?"

"Yes, Madam."

"You will inform Lisa that she is to be whipped every day, by one or the other of us. Immediately."

"Madam, please..."

"You speak out of turn, Carla!"

"I...Madam, please don't do this. Don't make me do this. She is too weak...."

"She will beg you to do it, won't she, Carla? Beg you with tears flowing to be the one, not me. And you will feel the excitement and the hate and every day you will feel it grow strong. You will want to hurt her, want to see blood spot her bare back. And your hate will grow until you won't be able to look at her without being blinded by your own hatred. You see, I know, Carla. I know all of it."

Carla stared at her in horror. "I won't do it. I won't."

"I will."

They were old and full of hatred for the shiny young faces, the bright hair, the straight backs and strong legs and arms. They said: let us remake them in our image and they did.

Carla repeated Madam Trudeau's words to the girls gathered in the two sleeping rooms on the third floor. Lisa swayed and was supported by Ruthie. Helga smiled.

That evening Ruthie tried to run away and was caught by two of the blue-clad Males. The girls were lined up and watched as Ruthie was stoned. They buried her without a service on the hill where she had been caught.

After dark, lying on the cot open-eyed, tense, Carla heard Lisa's whisper close to her ear. "I don't care if you hit me, Carla. It won't hurt like it does when she hits me."

"Go to bed, Lisa. Go to sleep."

"I can't sleep. I keep seeing Ruthie. I should have gone with her. I wanted to, but she wouldn't let me. She was afraid there would be Males on the hill watching. She said if she didn't get caught, then I should try to follow her at night." The child's voice was flat, as if shock had dulled her sensibilities.

Carla kept seeing Ruthie too. Over and over she repeated to herself: I should have tried it. I'm cleverer than she was. I might have escaped. I should have been the one. She knew it was too late now. They would be watching too closely.

An eternity later she crept from her bed and dressed quietly. Soundlessly she gathered her own belongings, and then collected the notebooks of the other girls, and the pens, and she left the room. There were dim lights on throughout the house as she made her way silently down stairs and through corridors. She left a pen by one of the outside doors, and very cautiously made her way back to the tiny space between the floors. She slid the door open and deposited everything else she carried inside the cave. She tried to get to the kitchen for food, but stopped when she saw one of the Officers of Law. She returned soundlessly to the attic rooms and tiptoed among the beds to Lisa's cot. She placed one hand over the girl's mouth and shook her awake with the other.

Lisa bolted upright, terrified, her body stiffened convulsively. With her mouth against the girl's ear Carla whispered, "Don't make a sound. Come on." She half led, half carried the girl to the doorway, down the stairs, and into the cave and closed the door.

"You can't talk here, either," she whispered. "They can hear." She spread out the extra garments she had collected and they lay down together, her arms tight about the girl's shoulders. "Try to sleep," she whispered. "I don't think they'll find us here. And after they leave, we'll creep out and live in the woods. We'll eat nuts and berries..."

The first day they were jubilant at their success and they giggled and muffled the noise with their skirts. They could hear all the orders being issued by Madam Trudeau: guards in all the halls, on the stairs, at the door to the dorm to keep other girls from trying to escape also. They could hear all the interrogations, of the girls, the guards who had not seen the escapees. They heard the mocking voice of the Doctor of Law deriding Madam Trudeau's boasts of absolute control.

The second day Carla tried to steal food for them, and, more important, water. There were blue-clad Males everywhere. She returned emptyhanded. During the night Lisa whimpered in her sleep and Carla had to stay awake to quiet the child, who was slightly feverish.

"You won't let her get me, will you?" she begged over and over.

The third day Lisa became too quiet. She didn't want Carla to move from her side at all. She held Carla's hand in her hot, dry hand and now and then tried to raise it to her face, but she was too weak now. Carla stroked her forehead.

When the child slept Carla wrote in the notebooks, in the dark, not knowing if she wrote over other words or on blank pages. She wrote her life story, and then made up other things to say. She wrote her name over and over, and wept because she had no last name. She wrote nonsense words and rhymed them with other nonsense words. She wrote of the savages who had laughed at the funeral and she hoped they wouldn't all die over the winter months. She thought that probably they would. She wrote of the golden light through green-black pine trees and of birds' songs and moss underfoot. She wrote of Lisa lying peacefully now at the far end of the cave amidst riches that neither of them could ever have comprehended. When she could no longer write, she drifted in and out of the golden light in the forest, listening to the birds' songs, hearing the raucous laughter that now sounded so beautiful.

THE BOOK

Michael Shaara

In ALPHA 7 we offered one of the science-fiction stories that Michael Shaara was writing a couple of decades before his Pulitzer-prize-winning novel *The Killer Angels*. And now another, closely related in theme to the first, examining in haunting fashion the problem of human (or inhuman) relations in a situation of total dreadful isolation.

Beauclaire was given his first ship at Sirius. He was called up before the Commandant in the slow heat of the afternoon, and stood shuffling with awkward delight upon the shaggy carpet. He was twenty-five years old, and two months out of the Academy. It was a wonderful day.

The Commandant told Beauclaire to sit down, and sat

looking at him for a long while. The Commandant was an old man with a face of many lines. He was old, was hot, was tired. He was also very irritated. He had reached that point of oldness when talking to a young man is an irritation because they are so bright and certain and don't know anything and there is nothing you can do about it.

"All right," the Commandant said, "there are a few things I have to tell you. Do you know where you are going?"

"No, sir," Beauclaire said cheerfully.

"All right," the Commandant said again, "I'll tell you. You are going to the Hole in Cygnus. You've heard of it, I hope? Good. Then you know that the Hole is a large dust cloud— estimated diameter, ten light-years. We have never gone into the Hole, for a number of reasons. It's too thick for light speeds, it's too big, and Mapping Command ships are being spread thin. Also, until now, we never thought there was anything in the Hole worth looking at. So we have never gone into the Hole. Your ship will be the first."

"Yes, *sir*," Beauclaire said, eyes shining.

"A few weeks ago," the Commandant said, "one of our amateurs had a lens on the Hole, just looking. He saw a glow. He reported to us: we checked and saw the same thing. There is a faint light coming out of the Hole—obviously a sun, a star inside the cloud, just far enough in to be almost invisible. God knows how long it's been there, but we do know that there's never been a record of light in the Hole. Apparently this star orbited in some time ago, and is now on its way out. It is just approaching the edge of the cloud. Do you follow me?"

"Yes, sir," Beauclaire said.

"Your job is this: You will investigate that sun for livable planets and alien life. If you find anything—which is highly unlikely—you are to decipher the language and come right back. A Psych team will go out and determine the effects of a starless sky upon the alien culture—obviously, these people will never have seen the stars."

The Commandant leaned forward, intent now for the first time.

"Now, this is an important job. There were no other linguists available, so we passed over a lot of good men to pick you. Make

95

no mistake about your qualifications. You are nothing spectacular. But the ship will be yours from now on, permanently. Have you got that?"

The young man nodded, grinning from ear to ear.

"There is something else," the Commandant said, and abruptly he paused.

He gazed silently at Beauclaire—at the crisp gray uniform, the baby-slick cheek—and he thought fleetingly and bitterly of the Hole in Cygnus which he, an old man, would never see. Then he told himself sternly to leave off self-pity. The important thing was coming up, and he would have to say it well.

"Listen," he said. The tone of his voice was very strong and Beauclaire blinked. "You are replacing one of our oldest men. One of our best men. His name is Billy Wyatt. He—he has been with us a long time." The Commandant paused again, his fingers toying with the blotter on his desk. "They have told you a lot of stuff at the Academy, which is all very important. But I want you to understand something else: This Mapping Command is a weary business—few men last for any length of time, and those that do aren't much good in the end. You know that. Well, I want you to be very careful when you talk to Billy Wyatt; and I want you to listen to him, because he's been around longer than anybody. We're relieving him, yes, because he is breaking down. He's no good for us any more; he has no more nerve. He's lost the feeling a man has to have to do his job right."

The Commandant got up slowly and walked around in front of Beauclaire, looking into his eyes.

"When you relieve Wyatt, treat him with respect. He's been farther and seen more than any man you will ever meet. I want no cracks and no pity for that man. Because, listen, boy, sooner or later the same thing will happen to you. Why? Because it's too big—" the Commandant gestured helplessly with spread hands—"it's all just too damn big. Space is never so big that it can't get bigger. If you fly long enough, it will finally get too big to make any sense, and you'll start thinking. You'll start thinking that it doesn't make sense. On that day, we'll bring you back and put you into an office somewhere. If we leave you alone, you lose ships and get good men killed—there's nothing we can do when space gets too big. That is what happened to Wyatt. That is what will happen, eventually, to you. Do you understand?"

The young man nodded uncertainly.

"And that," the Commandant said sadly, "is the lesson for today. Take your ship. Wyatt will go with you on this one trip, to break you in. Pay attention to what he has to say—it will mean something. There's one other crewman, a man named Cooper. You'll be flying with him now. Keep your ears open and your mouth shut, except for questions. And don't take any chances. That's all."

Beauclaire saluted and rose to go.

"When you see Wyatt," the Commandant said, "tell him I won't be able to make it down before you leave. Too busy. Got papers to sign. Got more damn papers than the chief has ulcers."

The young man waited.

"That, God help you, is all," said the Commandant.

Wyatt saw the letter when the young man was still a long way off. The white caught his eye, and he watched idly for a moment. And then he saw the fresh green gear on the man's back and the look on his face as he came up the ladder, and Wyatt stopped breathing.

He stood for a moment blinking in the sun. *Me?* he thought... *me?*

Beauclaire reached the platform and threw down his gear, thinking that this was one hell of a way to begin a career.

Wyatt nodded to him, but didn't say anything. He accepted the letter, opened it and read it. He was a short man, thick and dark and very powerful. The lines of his face did not change as he read the letter.

"Well," he said when he was done, "thank you."

There was a long wait, and Wyatt said at last: "Is the Commandant coming down?"

"No, sir. He said he was tied up. He said to give you his best."

"That's nice," Wyatt said.

After that, neither of them spoke. Wyatt showed the new man to his room and wished him good luck. Then he went back to his cabin and sat down to think.

After 28 years in the Mapping Command, he had become necessarily immune to surprise; he could understand this at once, but it would be some time before he would react. *Well, well,* he said to himself; but he did not feel it.

Vaguely, flicking cigarettes onto the floor, he wondered *why*.

97

The letter had not given a reason. He had probably flunked a physical. Or a mental. One or the other, each good enough reason. He was 47 years old, and this was a rough business. Still, he felt strong and cautious, and he knew he was not afraid. He felt good for a long while yet . . . but obviously he was not.

Well, then, he thought, *where now?*

He considered that with interest. There was no particular place for him to go. Really no place. He had come into the business easily and naturally, knowing what he wanted—which was simply to move and listen and see. When he was young, it had been adventure alone that drew him; now it was something else he could not define, but a thing he knew he needed badly. He had to see, to watch . . . and *understand.*

It was ending, the long time was ending. It didn't matter what was wrong with him. The point was that he was through. The point was that he was going home, to nowhere in particular.

When evening came, he was still in his room. Eventually he'd been able to accept it all and examine it clearly, and had decided that there was nothing to do. If there was anything out in space which he had not yet found, he would not be likely to need it.

He left off sitting, and went up to the control room.

Cooper was waiting for him.

Cooper was a tall, bearded, scrawny man with a great temper and a great heart and a small capacity for liquor. He was sitting all alone in the room when Wyatt entered.

Except for the pearl-green glow of dashlights from the panel, the room was dark. Cooper was lying far back in the pilot's seat, his feet propped up on the panel. One shoe was off, and he was carefully pressing buttons with his huge bare toes. The first thing Wyatt saw when he entered was the foot glowing luridly in the green light of the panel. Deep within the ship he could hear the hum of the dynamos starting and stopping.

Wyatt grinned. From the play of Coop's toes, and the attitude, and the limp, forgotten pole of an arm which hung down loosely from the chair, it was obvious that Coop was drunk. In port, he was usually drunk. He was a lean, likable man with very few cares, and no manners at all, which was typical of men in that Command.

"What say, Billy?" Coop mumbled from deep in the seat.

Wyatt sat down. "Where you been?"

"In the port. Been drinkin' in the goddamn port. Hot!"

"Bring back any?"

Coop waved an arm floppily in no particular direction. "Look around."

The flasks lay in a heap by the door. Wyatt took one and sat down again. The room was warm and green and silent. The two men had been together long enough to be able to sit without speaking, and in the green glow they waited, thinking. The first pull Wyatt took was long and numbing; he closed his eyes.

Coop did not move at all. Not even his toes. When Wyatt had begun to think he was asleep, he said suddenly:

"Heard about the replacement."

Wyatt looked at him.

"Found out this afternoon," Coop said, "from the goddam Commandant."

Wyatt closed his eyes again.

"Where you goin'?" Coop asked.

Wyatt shrugged. "Plush job."

"You got any plans?"

Wyatt shook his head.

Coop swore moodily. "Never let you alone," he muttered. "Miserable bastards." He rose up suddenly in the chair, pointing a long matchstick finger into Wyatt's face. "Listen, Billy," he said with determination, "you was a good man, you know that? You was one hell of a good goddam man."

Wyatt took another long pull and nodded, smiling.

"You said it," he said.

"I sailed with some good men, some *good* men," Coop insisted, stabbing shakily but emphatically with his finger, "but you don't take nothin' from nobody."

"Here's to me, I'm true blue," Wyatt grinned.

Coop sank back in the chair, satisfied. "I just wanted you should know. You been a good man."

"Betcher sweet life," Wyatt said.

"So they throw you out. *Me* they keep. *You* they throw out. They got no brains."

Wyatt lay back, letting the liquor take hold, receding without pain into a quiet world. The ship was good to feel around him, dark and throbbing like a living womb. *Just like a womb*, he thought. *It's a lot like a womb.*

"Listen," Coop said thickly, rising from his chair. "I think I'll quit this racket. What the hell I wanna stay in this racket for?"

Wyatt looked up, startled. When Coop was drunk, he was never a little drunk, He was always far gone, and he could be very mean. Wyatt saw now that he was down deep and sinking; that the replacement was a big thing to him, bigger than Wyatt had expected. In this team, Wyatt had been the leader, and it had seldom occurred to him that Coop really needed him. He had never really thought about it. But now he let himself realize that, alone, Coop could be very bad. Unless this new man was worth anything and learned quickly, Coop would very likely get himself killed.

Now, more than ever, this replacement thing was ridiculous; but for Coop's sake, Wyatt said quickly:

"Drop that, man. You'll be on this ship in the boneyard. You even look like this ship—you got a bright red bow."

When the tall man was dark and silent, Wyatt said gently, "Coop. Easy. We leave at midnight. Want me to take her up?"

"Naw." Coop turned away away abruptly, shaking his head. "T'hell with you. Go die." He sank back deeply in the seat, his gaunt face reflecting the green glow from the panel. His next words were sad, and, to Wyatt, very touching.

"Hell, Billy," Coop said wearily, "this ain' no fun."

Wyatt let him take the ship up alone. There was no reason to argue about it. Coop was drunk; his mind was unreachable.

At midnight, the ship bucked and heaved and leaped up into the sky. Wyatt hung tenuously to a stanchion by a port, watched the night lights recede and the stars begin blooming. In a few moments the last clouds were past, and they were out in the long night, and the million million speckled points of glittering blue and red and silver burned once more with the mighty light which was, to Wyatt, all that was real or had ever meant living. In the great glare and the black he stood, as always, waiting for something to happen, for the huge lonely beauty to resolve itself to a pattern and descend and be understood.

It did not. It was just space, an area in which things existed, in which mechanized substance moved. Wondering, waiting, Wyatt regarded the Universe. The stars looked icily back.

At last, almost completely broken, Wyatt went to bed.

* * *

Beauclaire's first days passed very quickly. He spent them in combing the ship, seeking her out in her deepest layers, watching and touching and loving. The ship was to him like a woman; the first few days were his honeymoon. Because there is no lonelier job that a man can have, it was nearly always this way with men in the Command.

Wyatt and Cooper left him pretty much alone. They did not come looking for him, and the few times that he did see them he could not help but feel their surprise and resentment. Wyatt was always polite. Cooper was not. Neither seemed to have anything to say to Beauclaire, and he was wise enough to stay by himself. Most of Beauclaire's life until now had been spent among books and dust and dead, ancient languages. He was by nature a solitary man, and therefore it was not difficult for him to be alone.

On a morning some weeks after the trip began, Wyatt came looking for him. His eyes twinkling, Wyatt fished him up, greasecoated and embarrassed, out of a shaft between the main dynamos. Together they went up toward the astrogation dome. And under the great dome, beneath the massive crystal sheet on the other side of which there was nothing for ever and ever, Beauclaire saw a beauty which he was to remember as long as he lived.

They were nearing the Hole in Cygnus. On the side which faces the center of the Galaxy, the Hole is almost flat, from top to bottom, like a wall. They were moving in on the flat side now, floating along some distance from the wall, which was so huge and incredible that Beauclaire was struck dumb.

It began above him, light-years high. It came down in a black, folding, rushing silence, fell away beneath him for millions upon millions of miles, passed down beyond sight so far away, so unbelievably far away and so vast, that there could be nothing as big as this, and if he had not seen the stars still blazing on either side he would have had to believe that the wall was just outside the glass, so close he could touch it. From all over the wall a haze reflected faintly, so that the wall stood out in ridges and folds from the great black of space. Beauclaire looked up and then down, and then stood and gazed.

After a while, Wyatt pointed silently down. Beauclaire

looked in among the folds and saw it, the tiny yellow gleam toward which they were moving. It was so small against the massive cloud that he lost it easily.

Each time he took his eyes away, he lost it, and had to search for it again.

"It's not too far in," Wyatt said at last, breaking the silence. "We'll move down the cloud to the nearest point, then we'll slow down and move in. Should take a couple of days."

Beauclaire nodded.

"Thought you'd like to see," Wyatt said.

"Thanks." Beauclaire was sincerely grateful. And then, unable to contain himself, he shook his head with wonder. "My God!" he said.

Wyatt smiled. "It's a big show."

Later, much later, Beauclaire began to remember what the Commandant had said about Wyatt. But he could not understand it at all. Sure, something like the Hole was incomprehensible. It did not make any sense—but so what? A thing as beautiful as that, Beauclaire thought, did not *have* to make sense.

They reached the sun slowly.

The gas was not thick by any Earthly standards—approximately one atom to every cubic mile of space—but for a starship, any matter at all is too much. At normal speeds, the ship would hit the gas like a wall. So they came in slowly, swung in and around the large yellow sun.

They saw one planet almost immediately. While moving in toward that one they scanned for others, found none at all.

Space around them was absolutely strange; there was nothing in the sky but a faint haze. They were in the cloud now, and of course could see no star. There was nothing but the huge sun and the green gleaming dot of that one planet, and the endless haze.

From a good distance out, Wyatt and Cooper ran through the standard tests while Beauclaire watched with grave delight. They checked for radio signals, found none. The spectrum of the planet revealed strong oxygen and water-vapor lines, surprisingly little nitrogen. The temperature, while somewhat cool, was in the livable range.

It was a habitable planet.

"Jackpot!" Coop said cheerfully. "All that oxygen, bound to be some kind of life."

Wyatt said nothing. He was sitting in the pilot chair, his huge hands on the controls, nursing the ship around into the long slow spiral which would take them down. He was thinking of many other things, many other landings. He was remembering the acid ocean at Lupus and the rotting disease of Altair, all the dark, vicious, unknowable things he had approached, unsuspecting, down the years.

. . . So many years, that now he suddenly realized it was too long, too long.

Cooper, grinning unconsciously as he scanned with the telescope, did not notice Wyatt's sudden freeze.

It was over all at once. Wyatt's knuckles had gradually whitened as he gripped the panel. Sweat had formed on his face and run down into his eyes, and he blinked, and realized with a strange numbness that he was soaking wet all over. In that moment, his hands froze and gripped the panel, and he could not move them.

It was a hell of thing to happen on a man's last trip, he thought. He would like to have taken her down just this once. He sat looking at his hands. Gradually, calmly, carefully, with a cold will and a welling sadness, he broke his hands away from the panel.

"Coop," he said, "take over."

Coop glanced over and saw. Wyatt's face was white and glistening; his hands in front of him were wooden and strange.

"Sure," Coop said, after a very long moment. "Sure."

Wyatt backed off, and Coop slid into the seat.

"They got me just in time," Wyatt said, looking at his stiff, still fingers. He looked up and ran into Beauclaire's wide eyes, and turned away from the open pity. Coop was bending over the panel, swallowing heavily.

"Well," Wyatt said. He was beginning to cry. He walked slowly from the room, his hands held before him like old gray things that had died.

The ship circled automatically throughout the night, while its crew slept or tried to. In the morning they were all forcefully cheerful and began to work up an interest.

There were people on the planet. Because the people lived in villages and had no cities and no apparent science, Coop let the ship land.

It was unreal. For a long while, none of them could get over the feeling of unreality, Wyatt least of all. He stayed in the ship and got briefly drunk, and then came out as carefully efficient as ever. Coop was gay and brittle. Only Beauclaire saw the planet with any degree of clarity. And all the while the people looked back.

From the very beginning it was peculiar.

The people saw the ship passing overhead, yet curiously they did not run. They gathered in groups and watched. When the ship landed, a small band of them came out of the circling woods and hills and ringed the ship, and a few came up and touched it calmly, ran fingers over smooth steel sides.

The people were human.

There was not, so far as Beauclaire could tell, a single significant difference. It was not really extraordinary—similar conditions will generally breed similar races—but there was something about these men and women which was hard and powerful, and in a way almost grand.

They were magnificently built, rounded and bronzed. Their women especially were remarkably beautiful. They were wearing woven clothes of various colors, in simple savage fashions; but there was nothing at all savage about them. They did not shout or seem nervous or move around very much, and nowhere among them was there any sign of a weapon. Furthermore, they did not seem to be particularly curious. The ring about the ship did not increase. Although several new people wandered in from time to time, others were leaving, unconcerned. The only ones among them who seemed at all excited were the children.

Beauclaire stood by the viewscreen, watching. Eventually Coop joined him, looking without interest until he saw the women. There was one particular girl with shaded brown eyes and a body of gentle hills. Coop grinned widely and turned up the magnification until the screen showed nothing but the girl. He was gazing with appreciation and making side comments to Beauclaire when Wyatt came in.

"Looka *that*, Billy," Coop roared with delight, pointing.

"Man, we have come home!"

Wyatt smiled very tightly, changed the magnification quickly to cover the whole throng around them.

"No trouble?"

"Nope," Coop said. "Air's good, too. Thin, but practically pure oxygen. Who's first to go out?"

"Me," Wyatt said, for obvious reasons. He would not be missed.

No one argued with him. Coop was smiling as Wyatt armed himself. Then he warned Wyatt to leave that cute little brown-eyed doll alone.

Wyatt went out.

The air was clear and cool. There was a faint breeze stirring the leaves around him, and Wyatt listened momentarily to the far bell-calls of birds This would be the last time he would ever go out like this, to walk upon an unknown world. He waited for some time by the airlock before he went forward.

The ring of people did not move as he approached, his hand upraised in what the Mapping Command had come to rely on as the universal gesture of peace. He paused before a tall, monolithic old man in a single sheath of green cloth.

"Hello," he said aloud, and bowed his head slowly.

From the ship, through the wide-angle sights of a gun, Beauclaire watched breathlessly as Wyatt went through the pantomime of greeting.

None of the tall people moved, except the old man, who folded his arms and looked openly amused. When the pantomime was done, Wyatt bowed again. The old man broke into a broad grin, looked amiably around at the circle of people, and then quite suddenly bowed to Wyatt. One by one the people, grinning, bowed.

Wyatt turned and waved at the ship, and Beauclaire stood away from his gun, smiling.

It was a very fine way to begin.

In the morning Wyatt went out alone, to walk in the sun among the trees, and he found the girl he had seen from the ship. She was sitting alone by a stream, her feet cooling and splashing in the clear water.

Wyatt sat down beside her. She looked up, unsurprised, out

of eyes that were rich and grained like small pieces of beautiful wood. Then she bowed, from the waist. Wyatt grinned and bowed back.

Unceremoniously he took off his boots and let his feet plunk down into the water. It was shockingly cold, and he whistled. The girl smiled at him. To his surprise, she began to hum softly. It was a pretty tune that he was able to follow, and after a moment he picked up the harmony and hummed along with her. She laughed, and he laughed with her, feeling very young.

Me Billy, he thought of saying, and laughed again. He was content just to sit without saying anything. Even her body, which was magnificent, did not move him to anything but a quiet admiration, and he regarded himself with wonder.

The girl picked up one of his boots and examined it critically, clucking with interest. Her lovely eyes widened as she played with the buckle. Wyatt showed her how the snaps worked and she was delighted and clapped her hands.

Wyatt brought other things out of his pockets and she examined them all, one after the other. The picture of him on his ID card was the only one which seemed to puzzle her. She handled it and looked at it, and then at him, and shook her head. Eventually she frowned and gave it definitely back to him. He got the impression that she thought it was very bad art. He chuckled.

The afternoon passed quickly, and the sun began to go down. They hummed some more and sang songs to each other which neither understood and both enjoyed, and it did not occur to Wyatt until much later how little curiosity they had felt. They did not speak at all. She had no interest in his language or his name, and, strangely, he felt all through the afternoon that talking was unnecessary. It was a very rare day spent between two people who were not curious and did not want anything from each other. The only words they said to each other were goodbye.

Wyatt, lost inside himself, plodding, went back to the ship.

In the first week, Beauclaire spent his every waking hour learning the language of the planet. From the very beginning he had felt an unsettling, peculiar manner about these people. Their behavior was decidedly unusual. Although they did not differ in

106

any appreciable way from human beings, they did not act very much like human beings in that they were almost wholly lacking a sense of awe, a sense of wonder. Only the children seemed surprised that the ship had landed, and only the children hung around and inspected it. Almost all the others went off about their regular business—which seemed to be farming—and when Beauclaire tried learning the language, he found very few of the people willing to spend time enought to teach him.

But they were always more or less polite, and by making a pest of himself he began to succeed. On another day when Wyatt came back from the brown-eyed girl, Beauclaire reported some progress.

"It's a beautiful language," he said as Wyatt came in. "Amazingly well-developed. It's something like our Latin—same type of construction, but much softer and more flexible. I've been trying to read their book."

Wyatt sat down thoughtfully and lit a cigarette.

"Book?" he said.

"Yes. They have a lot of books, but *everybody* has this one particular book—they keep it in a place of honor in their houses. I've tried to ask them what it is—I think it's a bible of some kind—but they just won't bother to tell me."

Wyatt shrugged, his mind drifting away.

"I just don't understand them," Beauclaire said plaintively, glad to have someone to talk to. "I don't get them at all. They're quick, they're bright, but they haven't the damnedest bit of curiosity about *anything,* not even each other. My God, they don't even gossip!"

Wyatt, contented, puffed quietly. "Do you think not seeing the stars has something to do with it? Ought to have slowed down the development of physics and math."

Beauclaire shook his head. "No. It's very strange. There's something else. Have you noticed the way the ground seems to be sharp and jagged almost everywhere you look, sort of chewed up as if there was a war? Yet these people swear that they've never had a war within living memory, and they don't keep any history so a man could really find out."

When Wyatt didn't say anything, he went on:

"And I can't see the connection about no stars. Not with these people. I don't care if you can't see the roof of the house you live in, you still have to have a certain amount of curiosity in order to stay alive. But these people just don't give a damn. The ship landed. You remember that? Out of the sky come Gods like thunder—"

Wyatt smiled. At another time, at any time in the past, he would have been very much interested in this sort of thing. But now he was not. He felt himself—remote, sort of—and he, like these people, did not particularly give a damn.

But the problem bothered Beauclaire, who was new and fresh and looking for reasons, and it also bothered Cooper.

"Damn!" Coop grumbled as he came stalking into the room. "Here you are, Billy. I'm bored stiff. Been all over this whole crummy place lookin for you. Where you been?" He folded himself into a chair, scratched his black hair broodingly with long, sharp fingers. "Game o' cards?"

"Not just now, Coop," Wyatt said, lying back and resting.

Coop grunted. "Nothin to do, nothin to do." he swiveled his eyes to Beauclaire. "How you comin, son? How soon we leave this place? Like Sunday afternoon all the time."

Beauclaire was always ready to talk about the problem. He outlined it now to Cooper again, and Wyatt, listening, grew very tired. There is just this one continent, Beauclaire said, and just one nation, and everyone spoke the same tongue. There was no government, no police, no law that he could find. There was not even, as far as he could tell, a system of marriage. You couldn't even call it a society, really, but dammit, it existed—and Beauclaire could not find a single trace of rape or murder or violence of any kind. The people here, he said, just didn't give a damn.

"You said it," Coop boomed. "I think they're all whacky."

"But happy," Wyatt said suddenly. "You can see that they're happy."

"Sure, they're happy," Coop chortled. "They're nuts. They got funny looks in their eyes. Happiest guys I know are screwy as—"

The sound which cut him off, which grew and blossomed and eventually explained everything, had begun a few seconds ago, too softly to be heard. Now suddenly, from a slight rushing noise, it burst into an enormous, thundering scream.

They leaped up together, horrified, and an overwhelming, gigantic blast threw them to the floor.

The ground rocked, the ship fluttered and settled crazily. In that one long second, the monstrous noise of a world collapsing grew in the air and filled the room, filled the men and everything with one incredible crushing, grinding shock.

When it was over there was another rushing sound, farther away, and another, and two more tremendous explosions; and though all in all the noise lasted for perhaps five seconds, it was the greatest any of them had ever heard, and the world beneath them continued to flutter, wounded and trembling, for several minutes.

Wyatt was first out of the ship, shaking his head as he ran to get back his hearing. To the west, over a long slight rise of green and yellow trees, a vast black cloud of smoke, several miles long and very high, was rising and boiling. As he stared and tried to steady his feet upon the shaking ground, he was able to gather himself enough to realize what this was.

Meteors.

He had heard meteors before, long before, on a world of Aldebaran. Now he could smell the same sharp burning disaster, and feel the wind rushing wildly back to the west, where the meteors had struck and hurled the air away.

In that moment Wyatt thought of the girl, and although she meant nothing to him at all—none of these people meant anything in the least to him—he began running as fast as he could toward the west.

Behind him, white-faced and bewildered, came Beauclaire and Cooper.

When Wyatt reached the top of the rise, the great cloud covered the whole valley before him. Fires were burning in the crushed forest to his right, and from the lay of the cloud he could tell that the village of the people was not there any more.

He ran down into the smoke, circling toward the woods and the stream where he had passed an afternoon with the girl. For a while he lost himself in the smoke, stumbling over rocks and fallen trees.

Gradually the smoke lifted, and he began running into some of the people. Now he wished that he could speak the language.

They were all wandering quietly away from the site of their village, none of them looking back. Wyatt could see a great many dead as he moved, but he had no time to stop, no time to wonder. It was twilight now, and the sun was gone. He thanked

God that he had a flashlight with him; long after night came, he
was searching in the raw gash where the first meteor had fallen.

He found the girl, dazed and bleeding, in a cleft between two
rocks. He knelt and took her in his arms. Gently, gratefully,
through the night and the fires and past the broken and the dead,
he carried her back to the ship.

It had all become frighteningly clear to Beauclaire. He talked
with the people and began to understand.

The meteors had been falling since the beginning of time, so
the people said. Perhaps it was the fault of the great dust-cloud
through which this planet was moving; perhaps it was that this
had not always been a one-planet system—a number of other
planets, broken and shredded by unknown gravitational forces,
would provide enough meteors for a very long time. And the air
of this planet being thin, there was no real protection as there
was on Earth. So year after year the meteors fell. In
unpredictable places, at unknowable times, the meteors fell, like
stones from the sling of God. They had been falling since the
beginning of time. So the people, the unconcerned people, said.

And here was Beauclaire's clue. Terrified and shaken as he
was, Beauclaire was the kind of man who saw reason in
everything. He followed this one to the end.

In the meantime, Wyatt nursed the girl. She had not been
badly hurt, and recovered quickly. But her family and friends
were mostly dead now, and so she had no reason to leave the
ship.

Gradually Wyatt learned the language. The girl's name was
ridiculous when spoken in English, so he called her Donna,
which was something like her real name. She was, like all her
people, unconcerned about the meteors and her dead. She was
extraordinarily cheerful. Her features were classic, her cheeks
slim and smiling, her teeth perfect. In the joy and whiteness of
her, Wyatt saw each day what he had seen and known in his
mind on the day the meteors fell. Love to him was something
new. He was not sure whether or not he was in love, and he did
not care. He realized that he needed this girl and was at home
with her, could rest with her and talk with her, and watch her
walk and understand what beauty was; and in the ship in those
days a great peace began to settle over him.

When the girl was well again, Beauclaire was in the middle of translating the book—the bible-like book which all the people seemed to treasure so much. As his work progressed, a striking change began to come over him. He spent much time alone under the sky, watching the soft haze through which, very soon, the stars would begin to shine.

He tried to explain what he felt to Wyatt, but Wyatt had no time.

"But, Billy," Beauclaire said fervently, "do you see what these people go through? Do you see how they live?"

Wyatt nodded, but his eyes were on the girl as she sat listening dreamily to a recording of ancient music.

"They live every day waiting," Beauclaire said. "They have no idea what the meteors are. They don't know that there is anything else in the Universe but their planet and their sun. They think that's all there is. They don't know why they're here—but when the meteors keep falling like that they have only one conclusion."

Wyatt turned from the girl smiling absently. None of this could touch him. He had seen the order and beauty of space, the incredible perfection of the Universe, so often and so deeply that, like Beauclaire, he could not help but believe in a Purpose, a grand final meaning. When his father had died of an insect bite at Oberon he had believed in a purpose for that, and had looked for it. When his first crewmate fell into the acid ocean of Alcestis and the second died of a horrible rot, Wyatt had seen purpose, purpose; and each time another man died, for no apparent reason, on windless, evil useless worlds, the meaning of things had become clearer and clearer, and now in the end Wyatt was approaching the truth, which was perhaps that none of it mattered at all.

It especially did not matter now. So many things had happened that he had lost the capacity to pay attention. He was not young any more; he wanted to rest, and upon the bosom of this girl he had all the reason for anything and everything he needed.

But Beauclaire was incoherent. It seemed to him that here on this planet a great wrong was being done, and the more he thought of it the more angry and confused he became. He went off by himself and looked at the terrible wound on the face of the

planet, at all the sweet, lovely, fragrant things which would
never be again, and he ended by cursing the nature of things, as
Wyatt had done so many years before. And then he went on with
the translation of the book. He came upon the final passage, still
cursing inwardly, and reread it again and again. When the sun
was rising on a brilliant new morning, he went back to the ship.

"They had a man here once," he said to Wyatt, "who was as
good a writer as there ever was. He wrote a book which these
people use as their Bible. It's like our Bible sometimes, but
mostly it's just the opposite. It preaches that a man shouldn't
worship anything. Would you like to hear some of it?"

Wyatt had been pinned down and he had to listen, feeling
sorry for Beauclaire, who had such a long way to go. His
thoughts were on Donna, who had gone out alone to walk in the
woods and say goodbye to her world. Soon he would go out and
bring her back to the ship, and she would probably cry a little,
but she would come. She would come with him always, wherever
he went.

"I have translated this the best way I could," Beauclaire said
thickly, "but remember this. This man could write. He was
Shakespeare and Voltaire and all the rest all at once. He could
make you *feel*. I couldn't do a decent translation if I tried
forever, but please listen and try to get what he means. I've put it
in the style of Ecclesiastes because it's something like that."

"All right," Wyatt said.

Beauclaire waited for a long moment, feeling this deeply.
When he read, his voice was warm and strong, and something of
his emotion came through. As Wyatt listened, he found his
attention attracted, and then he felt the last traces of his sadness
and weariness fall away.

He nodded, smiling.

These are the words Beauclaire had gathered from the Book:

Rise up smiling, and walk with me. Rise up in the
armor of thy body and what shall pass shall make thee
unafraid. Walk among the yellow hills, for they belong to
thee. Walk upon grass and let thy feet descend into soft
soil; in the end when all has failed thee the soil shall
comfort thee, the soil shall receive thee and in the dark bed
thou shalt find such peace as is thy portion.

In thine armor, hear my voice. In thine armor, hear.
Whatsoever thou does, thy friend and thy brother and thy
woman shall betray thee. Whatsoever thou dost plant, the
weeds and the seasons shall spite thee. Wheresoever thou
goest, the heavens shall fall upon thee. Though the
nations shall come unto thee in friendship thou art curst.
Know that the Gods ignore thee. Know that thou art Life,
and that pain shall forever come into thee, though thy
years be without end and thy days without sleep, even and
forever. And knowing this, in thine armor, thou shalt rise
up.

Red and full and glowing is thy heart; a steel is forging
within thy breast. And what can hurt thee now? In thy
granite mansion, what can hurt thee ever? Thou shalt only
die. Therefore seek not redemption nor forgiveness for
thy sins, for know that thou has never sinned.

Let the Gods come unto thee.

When it was finished, Wyatt sat very still.
Beauclaire was looking at him intently.
Wyatt nodded. "I see," he said.
"They don't ask for anything," Beauclaire said. "No
immortality, no forgiveness, no happiness. They take what
comes and don't—wonder."
Wyatt smiled, rising. He looked at Beauclaire for a long
while, trying to think of something to say. But there was nothing
to say. If the young man could believe this, here and now, he
would save himself a long, long, painful journey. But Wyatt
could not talk about it—not just yet.
He reached out and clapped Beauclaire gently upon the
shoulder. Then he left the ship and walked out toward the yellow
hills, toward the girl and the love that was waiting.

What will they do, Beauclaire asked himself, *when the stars
come out? When there are other places to go, will these people,
too, begin to seek?*
They would. With sadness, he knew that they would. For
there is a chord in Man which is plucked by the stars, which will
rise upward and outward into infinity, as long as there is one
man anywhere and one lonely place to which he has not been.

And therefore what does the meaning matter? We are built in this way and so shall we live.

Beauclaire looked up into the sky.

Dimly, faintly, like God's eye peeking through the silvery haze, a single star had begun to shine.

DUSTY ZEBRA

Clifford D. Simak

The Science Fiction Writers of America is not an organization noted for the sweet harmony of its opinions, but it has three times bestowed its Grand Master award with nary a murmur of dissent—to Robert A. Heinlein in 1975, to Jack Williamson in 1976, and, most recently, to Clifford D. Simak. All three are held in great affection by their fellow writers, but lovability is a secondary criterion in this business of handing out Grand Master trophies, and Simak, like the other two, received his block of lucite because of long and distinguished service to the craft and art of science fiction. For more than forty years he has delighted readers with ingenious, inviting, and unhurried stories. There is neither flash nor filigree to his manner, but what he writes sticks in the memory and sometimes in the soul. "Dusty Zebra" is Simak in fine form.

If you're human, you can't keep a thing around the house. You're always losing things and never finding them and you go charging through the place, yelling, cross-examining, blaming.

That's the way it is in all families.

Just one warning—don't try to figure out where all those things have gone or who might have taken them. If you have any notion of investigating, forget it. You'll be happier!

I'll tell you how it was with me.

I'd bought the sheet of stamps on my way home from the office so I could mail out the checks for the monthly bills. But I'd just sat down to write the checks when Marge and Lewis Shaw dropped over. I don't care much for Lewis and he barely tolerates me. But Marge and Helen are good friends, and they got to talking, and the Shaws stayed all evening.

Lewis told me about the work he was doing at his research laboratory out at the edge of town. I tried to switch him off to something else, but he kept right on. I suppose he's so interested in his work that he figures everyone else must be. But I don't know a thing about electronics and I can't tell a microgauge from a microscope.

It was a fairly dismal evening and the worst of it was that I couldn't say so. Helen would have jumped all over me for being antisocial.

So, the next evening after dinner, I went into the den to write the checks and, of course, the stamps were gone.

I had left the sheet on top of the desk and now the desk was bare except for one of the Bildo-Blocks that young Bill had outgrown several years before, but which still turn up every now and then in the most unlikely places.

I looked around the room. Just in case they might have blown off the desk, I got down on my hands and knees and searched under everything. There was no sign of the stamps.

I went into the living room, where Helen was curled up in a chair, watching television.

"I haven't seen them, Joe," she said. "They must be where you left them."

It was exactly the kind of answer I should have expected.

"Bill might know," I said.

"He's scarcely been in the house all day. When he does show up, you've got to speak to him."

"What's the matter now?"

"It's this trading business. He traded off that new belt we got him for a pair of spurs."

"I can't see anything wrong in that. When I was a kid . . ."

"It's not just the belt," she said. "He's traded everything. And the worst of it is that he always seems to get the best of it."

"The kid's smart."

"If you take that attitude, Joe . . ."

"It's not *my* attitude," I said. "It's the attitude of the whole business world. When Bill grows up . . ."

"When he grows up, he'll be in prison. Why, the way he trades, you'd swear he was training to be a con man!"

"All right, I'll talk to him."

I went back into the den because the atmosphere wasn't exactly as friendly as it might have been and, anyhow, I had to send out those checks, stamps or no stamps.

I got the pile of bills and the checkbook and the fountain pen out of the drawer. I reached out and picked up the Bildo-Block to put it to one side, so I'd have a good clear space to work on. But the moment I picked it up, I knew that this thing was no Bildo-Block.

It was the right size and weight and was black and felt like plastic, except that it was slicker than any plastic I had ever felt. It felt as if it had oil on it, only it didn't.

I set it down in front of me and pulled the desk lamp closer. But there wasn't much to see. It still looked like one of the Bildo-Blocks.

Turning it around, I tried to make out what it was. On the second turn, I saw the faint oblong depression along one side of it—a very shallow depression, almost like a scratch.

I looked at it a little closer and could see that the depression was machined and that within it was a faint red line. I could have sworn the red line flickered just a little. I held it there, studying it, and could detect no further flicker. Either the red had faded or I had been seeing things to start with, for after a few seconds I couldn't be sure there was any line at all.

I figured it must have been something Bill had picked up or traded for. The kid is more than half pack-rat, but there's nothing wrong with that, nor with the trading, either, for all that Helen says. It's just the first signs of good business sense.

I put the block over to one side of the desk and went on with the checks. The next day, during lunch hour, I bought some more stamps so I could mail them. And off and on, all day, I wondered what could have happened to that sheet of stamps.

I didn't think at all about the block that had the oily feel. Possibly I would have forgotten it entirely, except that when I got home, the fountain pen was missing

I went into the den to get the pen and there the pen was, lying on top of the desk where I'd left it the night before. Not that I remembered leaving it there. But when I saw it there, I remembered having forgotten to put it back into the drawer.

I picked it up. It wasn't any pen. It felt like a cylinder of cork, but much too heavy to be any kind of cork. Except that it was heavier and smaller, it felt something— somehow—like a fly rod.

Thinking of how a fly rod felt, I gave my hand a twitch, the way you do to cast a line, and suddenly it seemed to be, in fact, a fly rod. It apparently had been telescoped and now it came untelescoped and lengthened out into what might have been a rod. But the funny thing about it was that it went out only about four feet and then disappeared into thin air.

Instinctively, I brought it up and back to free the tip from wherever it might be. I felt the slack take up against a sudden weight and I knew I had something on the other end of it. Just like a fish feels, only it wasn't fighting.

Then, as quickly as it happened, it unhappened. I felt the tension snap off and the weight at the other end was gone and the rod had telescoped again and I held in my hand the thing that looked like a fountain pen.

I laid it down carefully on the desk, being very certain to make no more casting motions, and it wasn't until then that I saw my hand was shaking.

I sat down, goggling at the thing that looked like the missing fountain pen and the other thing that looked like a Bildo-Block.

And it was then, while I was looking at the two of them, that I saw, out of the corner of my eye, the little white dot in the center of the desk.

It was on the exact spot where the bogus pen had lain and more than likely, I imagined, the exact spot where I'd found the Bildo-Block the night before. It was about a quarter of an inch in diameter and it looked like ivory.

I put out my thumb and rubbed it vigorously, but the dot would not rub off. I closed my eyes so the dot would have a chance to go away, and then opened them again, real quick, to surprise it if it hadn't. It still was there.

I bent over the desk to examine it. I could see it was inlaid in the wood, and an excellent job of inlaying, too. I couldn't find even the faintest line of division between the wood and the dot.

It hadn't been there before; I was sure of that. If it had been, I would have noticed it. What's more, Helen would have noticed it, for she's hell on dirt and forever after things with a dusting cloth. And to cinch the fact that it had not been there before, no one I ever heard of sold desks with single inlaid ivory dots.

And no one sold a thing that looked like a fountain pen but could become a fly rod, the business end of which disappeared and hooked a thing you couldn't even see—and which, the next time, might bring in whatever it had caught instead of losing it.

Helen called to me from the living room. "Joe."

"Yeah. What is it?"

"Did you talk to Bill?"

"Bill? About what?"

"About the trading."

"No. I guess I forgot."

"Well, you'll have to. He's at it again. He traded Jimmy out of that new bicycle. Gave him a lot of junk. I made him give back the bicycle."

"I'll have a talk with him," I promised again.

But I'm afraid I wasn't paying as close attention to the ethics of the situation as I should have been.

You couldn't keep a thing around the house. You were always losing this or that. You knew just where you'd put it and you were sure it was there and then, when you went to look for it, it had disappeared.

It was happening everywhere—things being lost and never turning up.

But other things weren't left in their places—at least not that you heard about.

Although maybe there had been times when things had been left that a man might pick up and examine and not know what they were and puzzle over, then toss in a corner somewhere and forget.

Maybe, I thought, the junkyards of the world were loaded with outlandish blocks and crazy fishing rods.

I got up and went into the living room, where Helen had turned on the television set.

She must have seen that something had me upset, because she asked, "What's the matter now?"

"I can't find the fountain pen."

She laughed at me. "Honestly, Joe, you're the limit. You're always losing things."

That night, I lay awake after Helen went to sleep and all I could think about was the dot upon the desk. A dot, perhaps, that said: *Put it right here, pardner, and we will make a swap.*

And, thinking of it, I wondered what would happen if someone moved the desk.

I lay there for a long time, trying not to worry, trying to tell myself it didn't matter, that I was insane to think what I was thinking.

But I couldn't get it out of my mind.

So I finally got up and sneaked out of the bedroom and, feeling like a thief in my own house, headed for the den.

I closed the door, turned on the desk lamp and took a quick look to see if the dot was still there.

It was.

I opened the desk drawer and hunted for a pencil and couldn't find one, but I finally found one of Bill's crayons. I got down on my knees and carefully marked the floor around the desk legs, so that, if the desk were moved, I could put it back again.

Then, pretending I had no particular purpose for doing it, I laid the crayon precisely on the dot.

In the morning, I sneaked a look into the den and the crayon was still there. I went to work a little easier in my mind, for by then I'd managed to convince myself that it was all imagination.

But that evening, after dinner, I went back into the den and the crayon was gone.

In its place was a triangular contraption with what appeared to be lenses set in each angle, and with a framework of some sort of metal, holding in place what apparently was a suction cup in the center of the triangle.

While I was looking at it, Helen came to the door. "Marge and I are going to see a movie," she said. "Why don't you go over and have a beer with Lewis?"

"With that stuffed shirt?"

"What's the matter with Lewis?"

"Nothing, I guess." I didn't feel up to a family row right then.

"What's that you've got?" she asked.

"I don't know. Just something I found."

"Well, don't *you* start bringing home all sorts of junk, the way Bill does. One of you is enough to clutter up the house."

I sat there, looking at the triangle, and the only thing I could figure out was that it might be a pair of glasses. The suction cup in the center might hold it on the wearer's face and, while that might seem a funny way to wear a pair of glasses, it made sense when you thought about it. But if that were true, it meant that the wearer had three eyes, set in a triangle in his face.

I sat around for quite a while after Helen left, doing a lot of thinking. And what I was thinking was that even if I didn't care too much about Lewis, he was the only man I knew who might be able to help me out. So I put the bogus fountain pen and the three-eyed glasses in the drawer and put the counterfeit Bildo-Block in my pocket and went across the street.

Lewis had a bunch of blueprints spread out on the kitchen table, and he started to explain them to me. I did the best I could to act as if I understood them. Actually, I didn't know head nor tail of it.

Finally, I was able to get a word in edgewise and I pulled the block out of my pocket and put it on the table.

"What is that?" I asked.

I expected him to say right off it was just a child's block. But he didn't. There must have been something about it to tip him off that it wasn't just a simple block. That comes, of course, of having a technical education.

Lewis picked the block up and turned it around in his fingers. "What's it made of?" he asked me, sounding excited.

I shook my head. "I don't know what it is or what it's made of or anything about it. I just found it."

"This is something I've never seen before." Then he spotted the depression in one side of it and I could see I had him hooked. "Let me take it down to the shop. We'll see what we can learn."

I knew what he was after, of course. If the block was something new, he wanted a chance to go over it—but that didn't bother me any. I had a hunch he wouldn't find out too much about it.

We had a couple more beers and I went home. I hunted up an old pair of spectacles and put them on the desk right over the dot.

I was listening to the news when Helen came in. She said she was glad I'd spent the evening with Lewis, that I should try to get to know him better and that, once I got to know him better, I might like him. She said, since she and Marge were such good friends, it was a shame Lewis and I didn't hit it off.

"Maybe we will," I said and let it go at that.

The next afternoon, Lewis called me at the office.

"Where'd you get that thing?" he asked.

"Found it," I said.

"Have any idea what it is?"

"Nope," I told him cheerfully. "That's why I gave it to you."

"It's powered in some way and it's meant to measure something. That depression in the side must be a gauge. Color seems to be used as an indicator. At any rate, the color line in the depression keeps changing all the time. Not much, but enough so you can say there's some change."

"Next thing is to find out what it's measuring."

"Joe, do you know where you can get another of them?"

"No, I don't."

"It's this way," he said. "We'd like to get into this one, to see what makes it tick, but we can't find any way to open it. We could break into it, probably, but we're afraid to do that. We might damage it. Or it might explode. If we had another..."

"Sorry, Lewis. I don't know where to get another."

He had to let it go at that.

I went home that evening grinning to myself, thinking about Lewis. The guy was fit to be tied. He wouldn't sleep until he found out what the thing was, now that he'd started on it. It probably would keep him out of my hair for a week or so.

I went into the den. The glasses still were on the desk. I stood there for a moment, looking at them, wondering what was wrong. Then I saw that the lenses had a pinkish shade.

I picked them up, noticing that the lenses had been replaced by the kind in the triangular pair I had found there the night before.

Just then, Helen came into the room and I could tell, even before she spoke, that she had been waiting for me.

"Joe Adams," she demanded, "what have you been up to?"

"Not a thing," I told her.

"Marge says you got Lewis all upset."

"It doesn't take a lot to upset him."

"There's something going on," she insisted, "and I want to know what it is."

I knew I was licked. "I've been trading."

"Trading! After all I've said about Bill!"

"But this is different."

"Trading is trading," she said flatly.

Bill came in the front door, but he must have heard his mother say "trading," for he ducked out again. I yelled for him to come back.

"I want both of you to sit down and listen to me," I said. "You can ask questions and offer suggestions and give me hell after I'm through."

So we sat down, all three of us, and had a family pow-wow.

It took quite a bit to make Helen believe what I had to tell, but I pointed out the dot in the desk and showed them the triangular glasses and the pair of glasses that had been refitted with the pink lenses and sent back to me. By that time, she was ready to admit there was something going on. Even so, she was fairly well burned up at me for marking up the floor around the desk legs.

I didn't show either her or Bill the pen that was a fishing rod, for I was scared of that. Flourish it around a bit and there was no telling what would happen.

Bill was interested and excited, of course. This was trading, which was right down his alley.

I cautioned both of them not say a word about it. Bill wouldn't, for he was hell on secrets and special codes. But bright and early in the morning, Helen would probably swear Marge to secrecy, then tell her all about it and there wasn't a thing that I could do or say to stop her.

Bill wanted to put the pink-lensed spectacles on right away, to see how they were different from any other kind. I wouldn't let him. I wanted to put those specs on myself, but I was afraid to, if you want to know the truth.

When Helen went out to the kitchen to get dinner, Bill and I held a strategy session. For a ten-year-old, Bill had a lot of good ideas. We agreed that we ought to get some system into the trading, because, as Bill pointed out, the idea of swapping sight unseen was a risky sort of business. A fellow ought to have some say in what he was getting in return.

But to arrive at an understanding with whoever we were trading with meant that we'd have to set up some sort of communication system. And how do you communicate with someone you don't know the first thing about, except that perhaps it has three eyes?

Then Bill hit upon what seemed a right idea. What we needed, he said, was a catalogue. If you were going to trade with someone, the logical first step would be to let them know what you had to trade.

To be worth anything in such a circumstance, it would have to be an illustrated catalogue. And even then it might be worthless, for how could we be sure that the Trader on the other side of the desk would know what a picture was? Maybe he'd never seen a picture before. Maybe he saw differently—not so much physically, although that was possible, too, but from a different viewpoint and with totally alien concepts.

But it was the only thing we had to go on, so we settled down to work up a catalogue. Bill thought we should draw one, but neither of us was any good at drawing. I suggested illustrations from magazines. But that wasn't too hot an idea, either, for pictures of items in the magazine ads are usually all prettied up, designed to catch the eye.

Then Bill had a top-notch idea. "You know that kid dictionary Aunt Ethel gave me? Why don't we send that to them? It's got a lot of pictures and not much reading in it, and that's important. The reading might confuse them."

So we went into his room and started looking through all the junk he had, searching for the dictionary. But we ran across one of the old ABC books he'd had when he was just a toddler and decided it was even better than the dictionary. It had good clear pictures and almost no reading at all. You know the kind of book I mean— A for apple, B for ball and so forth.

We took the book into the den and put it on the desk, centering it on the dot, then went out to dinner.

In the morning the book had disappeared and that was a little odd. Up until then, nothing had disappeared from the desk until late in the day.

Early that afternoon, Lewis called me up. "I'm coming down to see you, Joe. Is there a bar handy where the two of us can be alone?"

I told him there was one only a block from me and said I'd meet him there.

I got a few things cleared away, then left the office, figuring I'd go over to the bar and have a quick one before Lewis showed up.

I don't know how he did it, but he was there ahead of me, back in a corner booth. He must have broken every traffic regulation on the books.

He had a couple of drinks waiting for us and was all huddled over, like a conspirator. He was a bit out of breath, as he had every right to be.

"Marge told me," he said.

"I suspected she would."

"There could be a mint in it, Joe!"

"That's what I thought, too. That's why I'm willing to give you ten per cent..."

"Now look here," squawked Lewis. "You can't pull a deal like that. I wouldn't touch it for less than fifty."

"I'm letting you in on it," I said, "because you're a neighbor. I don't know beans about this technical business. I'm getting stuff I don't understand and I need some help to find out what it is, but I can always go to someone else..."

It took us three drinks to get the details settled— 35 percent for him, 65 for me.

"Now that that's settled," I said, "suppose you tell me what you found."

"Found?"

"That block I gave you. You wouldn't have torn down here and had the drinks all set up and waiting if you hadn't found something."

"Well, as a matter of fact..."

"Now just a minute," I warned him. "We're going to put this in the contract—any failure to provide full and complete analysis..."

"What contract?"

"We're going to have a contract drawn up, so either of us can sue the other within an inch of his life for breaking it."

Which is a hell of a way to start out a business venture, but it's the only way to handle a slippery little skate like Lewis.

So he told me what he'd found. "It's an emotions gauge. That's awkward terminology, I know, but it's the best I can think of."

"What does it do?"

"It tells how happy you are or how sad or how much you hate someone."

"Oh, great," I said, disappointed. "What good is a thing like that? I don't need a gauge to tell me if I'm sore or glad or anything."

He waxed practically eloquent. "Don't you see what an instrument like that would mean to psychiatrists? It would tell more about patients than they'd ever be willing to tell about themselves. It could be used in mental institutions and it might be important in gauging reactions for the entertainment business, politics, law-enforcement and Lord knows knows what else."

"No kidding! Then let's start marketing!"

"The only thing is..."

"Yes?"

"We can't manufacture them," he said frustratedly. "We haven't got the materials and we don't know how they're made. You'll have to trade for them."

"I can't. Not right away, that is. First I've got to be able to make the Traders understand what I want, and then I'll have to find out what they're willing to trade them for."

"You have some other stuff?"

"A few things."

"You better turn them over to me."

"Some that could be dangerous. Anyhow, it all belongs to me. I'll give you what I want, when I want..."

We were off again.

We finally wound up by adjourning to an attorney's office. We wrote up a contract that is probably one of the legal curiosities of all time.

I'm convinced that attorney thought, and still thinks, both of us are crazy, but that's the least of my worries now.

The contract said I was to turn over to Lewis, for his determination of its technical and merchandisable nature, at least 90 per cent of certain items, the source of which I alone controlled, and with the further understanding that said source was to remain at all times under my exclusive control. The other 10 per cent might, without prejudice, be withheld from his examination, with the party of the first part having sole authority to make determination of which items should constitute the withheld 10 per cent.

Upon the 90 per cent of the items supplied him, the party of the second part was to make a detailed analysis, in writing, accompanied by such explanatory material as was necessary to the complete understanding of the party of the first part, within no more than three months after receipt, at the end of which time the items reverted solely to the ownership of the party of the first part. Except that such a period of examination and determination might be extended, under a mutual agreement made in writing, for any stated time.

Under no circumstances should the party of the second part conceal from the party of the first part any findings he might have made upon any of the items covered by the agreement, and that such concealment, should it occur, should be considered sufficient cause for action for the recovery of damages. That under certain conditions where some of the items might be found to be manufacturable, they could be manufactured under the terms of clauses A, B and C, section XII of this agreement.

Provisions for a sales organization to market any of said items shall be set up and made a part of this agreement. That any proceeds from such sales shall be divided as follows: 65 percent to the party of the first part (me, in case you've gotten lost, which is understandable), and 35 percent to the party of the second part (Lewis); costs to be apportioned accordingly.

There were a lot more details, of course, but that gives you an idea.

We got home from the attorney's office, without either of us knifing the other, and found Marge over at my place. Lewis went in with me to have a look at the desk.

Apparently the Trader had received the ABC book all right and had been able to understand why it was sent, for there, lying on the desk, was a picture cut out of the book. Well, not cut out exactly—it looked more as though it had been burned out.

The picture on the desk was Z for zebra.

Lewis stared worriedly at it. "Now we're really in a fix."

"Yeah," I admitted. " I don't know what the market price is, but they can't be cheap."

"Figure it out—expedition, safari, cages, ship, rail, fodder, keeper. You think we can switch him to something else?"

"I don't see how. He's put in his order."

Bill came wandering in and wanted to know what was up. When I glumly told him, he said cheerfully, "Aw, that's the whole trick in trading, Pop. If you got a bum jackknife you want to trade, you unload it on somebody who doesn't know what a good knife is like."

Lewis didn't get it, but I did. "That's right! He doesn't know a zebra is an animal, or if he does, how big it is!"

"Sure," Bill said confidently. "All he saw was a picture."

It was five o'clock then, but the three of us went uptown and shopped. Bill found a cheap bracelet charm about the size of the drawing in the book. When it comes to junk like that, my kid knows just where it's sold and how much it costs. I considered making him a junior partner in charge of such emergencies, with about 10 per cent share or so—out of Lewis's 35 per cent, of course—but I was sure Lewis wouldn't hold still for that. I decided instead to give Bill a dollar a week allowance, said compensation to commence immediately upon our showing a profit.

Well, we had Z for zebra—provided the Trader was satisfied with a little piece of costume jewelry. It was lucky, I thought, that it hadn't been Z for zephyr.

The rest of the alphabet was easy, yet I couldn't help but kick myself over all the time we were wasting. Of all the unworthy catalogues we might have sent, that ABC book was the worst. But until the Trader had run through the whole list, I was afraid to send another for fear of confusing him.

So I sent him an apple and a ball and a small doll for a girl and toy cat and toy dog, and so on, and then I lay awake nights wondering what the Trader would make of them. I could picture him trying to learn the use of a rubber doll or cat.

I'd given Lewis the two pairs of glasses, but had held back the fountain-pen fishing rod, for I was still scared of that one. He had turned over the emotion gauge to a psychiatrist to try out in his practice as a sort of field test.

Marge and Helen, knowing that Lewis and I had entered into some kind of partnership, were practically inseparable now. Helen kept telling me how glad she was that I had finally recognized what a sterling fellow Lewis was. I suppose Lewis heard the same thing about me from Marge.

Bill went around practically busting to do some bragging. But Bill is a great little businessman and he kept his mouth shut. I told him about the allowance, of course.

Lewis was all for trying to ask the Trader for a few more of the emotion gauges. He had a draftsman at the plant draw up a picture of the gauge and he wanted me to send it through to indicate that we were interested in it.

But I told him not to try to rush things. While the emotion gauge might be a good deal, we should sample what the Trader had to offer before we made up our minds.

The Trader, apparently certain now that someone was co-operating with him, had dropped his once-a-day trade schedule and was open for business around the clock. After he had run through the list in the ABC book, he sent back a couple of blank pages from the book with very crude drawings on them— drawings that looked as if they had been made with crumbly charcoal. Lewis drew a series of pictures, showing how a pencil worked, and we sent the Trader a ream of paper and a gross of sharpened pencils, then sat back to wait.

We waited a week and were getting sort of edgy, when back came the entire ream of paper, with each sheet covered on both sides with all kinds of drawings. So we sent him a mail-order catalogue, figuring that would hold him for a while, and settled down to try to puzzle out the drawings he had made.

There wasn't a single thing that made any sense at all—not even to Lewis. He'd study some of the drawings, then pace up and down the room, pulling his hair and twitching his ears. Then he'd study the drawing some more.

To me, it all looked plain Rube Goldbergish.

Finally, we figured we might as well forget about the catalogue idea, for the time being at least, and we started feeding all sorts of stuff through the desk—scissors, dishes, shoes, jackknives, mucilage, cigars, paper clips, erasers, spoons—almost anything that was handy. It wasn't the scientific way, I know, but we didn't have the time to get very methodical about it and, until we had a chance to work out a more sensible program, we figured we might as well try the shotgun method.

And the Trader started shooting things back at us. We'd sit for hours and feed stuff through to him and then he'd shoot stuff back at us and we had the damnedest pile of junk heaped all over the place you ever laid eyes on.

We rigged up a movie camera and took a lot of film of the spot on the desk where the exchange was going on. We spent a lot of time viewing that film, slowing it down and even stopping it, but it didn't tell us anything at all. When the stuff disappeared or appeared, it just disappeared or appeared. One frame it would be there, the next frame it would be gone.

Lewis canceled all his other work and used the lab for nothing but trying to puzzle out the gadgets that we got. Most of them we couldn't crack at all. I imagine they were useful in some way, but we never managed to learn how.

There was the perfume bottle, for example. That is what we called it, anyhow. But there was suspicion in our minds that the perfume was simply a secondary effect, that the so-called bottle was designed for some other purpose entirely.

Lewis and his boys were studying it down at the lab, trying to make out some rhyme or reason for it, and somehow they turned it on. They worked for three days, the last two in gas masks, trying to turn it off again. When the smell got so bad that people began calling the police, we took the contraption out into the country and buried it. Within a few day, all the vegetation in the area was dead. All the rest of the summer, the boys from the agricultural department at the university ran around, practically frothing at the mouth, trying to find the cause.

There was the thing that might have been a clock of some sort, although it might just as easily have been something else. If it was a clock, the Trader had a time system that would drive you nuts, for it would measure the minutes or hours or whatever they were like lightning for a while, then barely move for an entire day.

And there was the one you'd point at something and press a certain spot on it—not a button or a knob or anything as crass and mechanical as that, just a certain spot—and there'd be just a big blank spot in the landscape. But when you stopped pressing, the landscape would come back again, unchanged. We filed it away in the darkest corner of the laboratory safe, with a big red tag on it marked: *Dangerous! Don't Monkey with This!*

But most of the items we just drew blanks on. And it kept coming all the time. I piled the garage full of it and started dumping it in the basement. Some of it I was scared of and hauled out to the dump.

In the meantime, Lewis was having trouble with the emotion gauge. "It works," he said. "The psychiatrist I gave it to to try out is enthusiastic about it. But it seems almost impossible to get it on the market."

"If it works," I objected, handing him a can of beer, "it ought to sell."

"In any other field, it might, but you don't handle merchandise that way in the medical field. Before you can put something on the market, you have to have it nailed down with blueprints and theory and field tests and such. And we can't. We don't know *how* it works. We don't know *why* it works. Until we do, no reputable medical supply house will take it on, no approved medical journal will advertise it, no practitioner will use it."

"Then I guess it's out." I felt fairly blue about it, because it was the only thing we had that we knew how to use.

Lewis nodded and drank his beer and was glummer than ever.

Looking back on it, it's funny how we found the gadget that made us all the money. Actually, it wasn't Lewis but Helen who found it.

Helen is a good housewife. She's always going after things with the vacuum and the dustcloth and she washes the woodwork so often and so furiously that we have to paint it every year.

One night, we were sitting in the living room, watching television.

"Joe," she asked me, "did you dust the den?"

"Dust the den? What would I want to do that for?"

"Well, someone did. Maybe it was Bill."

131

"Bill wouldn't be caught dead with a dustcloth in his mitt."

"I can't understand it, Joe," she said. "I went in there to dust it and it was absolutely clean. Everything just shone."

Sgt. Friday was trying to get the facts out of someone and his sidekick was complaining about some relatives that had come to visit and I didn't pay much attention at the time.

But the next day, I got to thinking about it and I couldn't get it off my mind. I certainly hadn't dusted the den and it was a cinch Bill hadn't, yet someone had if Helen was ready to admit it was clean.

So, that evening, I went out into the street with a pail and shoveled up a pailful of dirt and brought it in the house.

Helen caught me as I was coming in the door. "What do you think you're doing with that?"

"Experimenting," I told her.

"Do it in the garage."

"It isn't possible," I argued. "I have to find out who's been dusting the den."

I knew that, if my hunch failed, I'd have a lot to answer for when she followed me and stood in the doorway, ready to pounce.

There was a bunch of junk from the Trader standing on the desk and a lot more of it in one corner. I cleared off the desk and that was when Bill came in.

"What you doing, Dad?" he asked.

"Your father's gone insane," Helen explained quietly.

They stood there, watching me, while I took a handful of dirt and sprinkled on the desk top.

It stayed there for just an instant—and then it was gone. The top of the desk was spotless.

"Bill," I said, "take one of those gadgets out to the garage."

"Which one?"

"It doesn't matter."

So he took one and I spread another handful of dirt and, in a second, it was gone.

Bill was back by that time and I sent him out with another gadget.

We kept on like that for quite a while and Bill was beginning to get disgusted with me. But finally I sprinkled the dirt and it stayed.

"Bill," I said, "you remember the last thing you took out?"

"Sure."

"Well, go out and bring it back again."

He got it and, as soon as he reached the door of the den, the dirt disappeared.

"Well, that's it," I said.

"That's what?" asked Helen.

I pointed to the contraption Bill had in his hand. "That. Throw away your vacuum cleaner. Burn up the dustcloth. Heave out the mop. Just have one of those in the house and ..."

She threw herself into my arms.

"Oh, *Joe!*"

We danced a jig, the two of us.

Then I sat around for a while, kicking myself for tying up with Lewis, wondering if maybe there wasn't some way I could break the contract now that I had found something without any help from him. But I remembered all those clauses we had written in. It wouldn't have been any use, anyhow, for Helen was already across the street, telling Marge about it.

So I phoned Lewis at the lab and he came tearing over.

We ran field tests.

The living room was spotless from Bill just having walked through it, carrying the gadget, and the garage, where he had taken it momentarily, was spic and span. While we didn't check it, I imagine that an area paralleling the path he had taken from the front door to the garage was the only place outdoors that didn't have a speck of dust upon it.

We took the gadget down in the basement and cleaned that up. We sneaked over to a neighbor's back yard, where we knew there was a lot of cement dust, held the gadget over it and in an instant there wasn't any cement dust. There were just a few pebbles left and the pebbles, I suppose, you couldn't rightly classify as dust.

We didn't need to know any more.

Back at the house, I broke open a bottle of Scotch I'd been saving, while Lewis sat down at the kitchen table and drew a sketch of the gadget.

We had a drink, then went into the den and put the drawing on the desk. The drawing disappeared and we waited. In a few minutes, another one of the gadgets appeared. We waited for a while and nothing happened.

"We've got to let him know we want a lot of them," I said.

"There's no way we can," said Lewis. "We don't know his mathematical symbols, he doesn't know ours, and there's no sure-fire way to teach him. He doesn't know a single word of our language and we don't know a word of his."

We went back to the kitchen and had another drink.

Lewis sat down and drew a row of the gadgets across a sheet of paper, then sketched in representations of others behind them so that, when you looked at it, you could see that there were hundreds of them.

We sent that through.

Fourteen gadgets came back—the exact number Lewis had sketched in the first row.

Apparently the Trader had no idea of perspective. The lines that Lewis had drawn to represent the other gadgets behind the first row didn't mean a thing to him.

We went back to the kitchen and had a few more drinks.

"We'll need thousands of the things," said Lewis, holding his head in his hands. "I can't sit here day and night, drawing them."

"You may have to do that," I said, enjoying myself.

"There *must* be another way."

"Why not draw a bunch of them, then mimeograph the drawing?" I suggested. "We could send the mimeograph sheets through to him in bundles."

I hated to say it, because I was still enamored of the idea of sticking Lewis somewhere off in a corner, sentenced to a lifetime of drawing the same thing over and over.

"That might work," said Lewis, brightening annoyingly. "It's just simple enough..."

"Practical is the word," I snapped. "If it were simple, you'd have thought of it."

"I leave things like that to detail men."

"You'd better!"

It took a while and a whole bottle before we calmed down.

Next day, we bought a mimeograph machine and Lewis drew a stencil with twenty-five of the gadgets on it. We ran through a hundred sheets and sent them through the desk.

It worked—we were busy for several hours, getting those gadgets out of the way as they poured through to us.

I'm afraid we never stopped to think about what the Trader

might want in return for the dust-collectors. We were so excited that we forgot, for the moment, that this was a commercial proposition and not just something gratis.

But the next afternoon, back came the mimeographed sheets we'd sent through and, on the reverse side of each of them, the Trader had drawn twenty-five representations of the zebra bracelet charm.

And there we were, faced with the necessity of getting together pronto, twenty-five hundred of those silly zebras.

I tore down to the store where I'd gotten the bracelet, but all they had in stock were two dozen of the things. They said they didn't think they could order any more. The number, they said, had been discontinued.

The name of the company that made them was stamped on the inside of the bracelet and, as soon as I got home, I put in a long distance call.

I finally got hold of the production manager. "You know those bracelets you put out?"

"We put out millions of 'em. Which one are you talking about?"

"The one with the zebra on it."

He thought a moment. "Yeah, we did. Quite a while ago. We don't make them any more. In this business..."

"I need at least twenty-five hundred of them."

"Twenty-five hundred bracelets?"

"No, just the zebras."

"Look, is this a gag?"

"It's no gag, mister," I said. "I need those zebras. I'm willing to pay for them."

"We haven't any in stock."

"Couldn't you make them?"

"Not just twenty-five hundred of them. Wouldn't be worth it to put through a special order for so few. If it was fifty-thousand, say, we might consider it."

"All right, then," I said. "How much for fifty thousand?"

He named a price and we haggled some, but I was in no position to do much bargaining. We finally agreed on a price I knew was way too high, considering the fact that the entire bracelet, with the zebra and a lot of other junk, had only retailed at 39 cents.

"And hold the order open," I told him. "We might want more of them."

"Okay," he said. "Just one thing—would you mind telling me what you want with fifty thousand zebras?"

"Yes, I would," I said and hung up.

I suppose he thought I was off my rocker, but who cared what he thought?

It took ten days to get that shipment of fifty thousand zebras and I sweated out every minute of it. Then there was a job of getting them under cover when it came and, in case you don't know, fifty thousand zebras, even when they're only bracelet charms, take up room.

But first I took out twenty-five hundred and sent them through the desk.

For the ten days since we'd gotten the dust-collectors, we'd sent nothing through and there had been no sign from the Trader that he might be getting impatient. I wouldn't have blamed him a bit if he'd done something, like sending through his equivalent of a bomb, to express his dissatisfaction at our slow delivery. I've often wondered what he thought of the long delay—if he hadn't suspected we were reneging on the bargain.

All the time, I had been smoking too much and gnawing my fingernails and I'd figured that Lewis was just as busy seeing what could be done about marketing the dusters.

But when I mentioned it to him he just looked blank. "You know, Joe, I've been doing a lot of worrying."

"We haven't a thing to worry about now," I said, "except getting these things sold."

"But the dust must go somewhere," he fretted.

"The dust?"

"Sure, the dust these things collect. Remember we picked up an entire pile of cement dust? What I want to know is where it all went. The gadget itself isn't big enough to hold it. It isn't big enough to hold even a week's collection of dust from the average house. That's what worries me—where does it go?"

"I don't care where. It goes, doesn't it?"

"That's the pragmatic view," he said scornfully.

It turned out that Lewis hadn't done a thing about marketing, so I got busy.

But I ran into the same trouble we'd had trying to sell the emotion gauge.

The dust-collector wasn't patented and it didn't have a brand name. There was no fancy label stuck on it and it didn't bear a manufacturer's imprint. And when anybody asked me how it worked, I couldn't answer.

One wholesaler did make me a ridiculous offer. I laughed in his face and walked out.

That night, Lewis and I sat around the kitchen table, drinking beer, and neither of us too happy. I could see a lot of trouble ahead in getting the gadgets sold. Lewis, it seemed, was still worrying about what happened to the dust.

He had taken one of the dust collectors apart and the only thing he could find out about it was that there was some feeble force-field operating inside of it—feeble yet strong enough to play hell with the electrical circuits and fancy metering machinery he has at the lab. As soon as he found out what was happening, he slapped the cover back on as quick as he could and then everything was all right. The cover was a shield against the force-field.

"That dust must be getting thrown into another dimension," he told me, looking like a hound dog that had lost a coon track.

"Maybe not. It could be winding up in one of those dust clouds way out in space."

He shook his head.

"You can't tell me," I said, "that the Trader is crazy enough to sell us a gadget that will throw dust back into his face."

"You miss the point entirely. The Trader is operating from another dimension. He *must* be. And if there are two dimensions, his and ours, there may be others. The Trader must have used these dust-collectors himself—not for the same purpose we intend, perhaps, but they get rid of something that he doesn't want around. So, necessarily, they'd have to be rigged to get rid of it in a dimension other than his."

We sat there drinking beer and I started turning over that business about different dimensions in my head. I couldn't grasp the concept. Maybe Lewis was right about me being a pragmatist. If you can't see it or touch it or even guess what it would be like, how can you believe there might be another dimension? I couldn't.

So I started to talk about marketing the dust-collector and before Lewis went home that night, we'd decided that the only thing left to do was sell it door to door. We even agreed to charge $12.50 for it. The zebras figured out to four cents each and we would pay our salesmen 10 per cent commission, which would leave us a profit of $11.21 apiece.

I put an ad in the paper for salesmen and the next day we had several applicants. We started them out on a trial run.

Those gadgets sold like hotcakes and we knew we were in!

I quit my job and settled down to handling the sales end, while Lewis went back to the lab and started going through the pile of junk we had gotten from the Trader.

There are a lot of headaches running a sales campaign. You have to map out territories for your salesmen, get clearance from Better Business Bureaus, bail out your men if they're thrown in the clink for running afoul of some obscure village ordinance. There are more worrisome angles to it than you can ever imagine.

But in a couple of months' time, things were running pretty smoothly. We had the state well covered and were branching into others. I had ordered another fifty thousand zebras and told them to expect re-orders—and the desk top was a busy place. It got to a point, finally, where I had to hire three men full time, paying them plenty not to talk, to man that desk top twenty-four hours a day. We'd send through zebras for eight hours, then take away dust gadgets for eight hours, then feed through zebras for another eight.

If the Trader had any qualms about what was happening, he gave no sign of it. He seemed perfectly happy to send us dust-collectors so long as we sent him zebras.

The neighbors were curious and somewhat upset at first, but finally they got used to it. If I could have moved to some other location, I would have, for the house was more an office than a home and we had practically no family life at all. But if we wanted to stay in business, we had to stay right where we were because it was the only place we had contact with the Trader.

The money kept rolling in and I turned the management of it over to Helen and Marge. The income tax boys gave us a rough time when we didn't show any manufacturing expenses, but since we weren't inclined to argue over what we had to pay, they couldn't do anything about it.

Lewis was wearing himself down to a nubbin at the lab, but he wasn't finding anything that we could use.

But he still did some worrying now and then about where all that dust was going. And he was right, probably for the first time in his life.

One afternoon, a couple of years after we'd started selling the dust-collectors, I had been uptown to attend to some banking difficulties that Helen and Marge had gotten all bollixed up. I'd no more than pulled into the driveway when Helen came busting out of the house. She was covered with dust, her face streaked with it, and she was the maddest-looking woman I have ever seen.

"You've got to do something about it, Joe!" she shrieked.

"About what?"

"The dust! It's pouring into the house!"

"Where is it pouring from?"

"From *everywhere*!"

I could see she'd opened all the windows and there was dust pouring out of them, almost like a smoke cloud. I got out of the car and took a quick look up and down the street. Every house in the block had its windows open and there was dust coming out of all of them and the neighborhood was boiling with angry, screaming women.

"Where's Bill?" I asked.

"Out back."

I ran around the house and called him and he came running.

Marge had come across the street and, if anything, she was about six degrees sorer about all the dust than Helen was.

"Get in the car," I said.

"Where are we going?" Marge demanded.

"Out to pick up Lewis."

I must have sounded like nothing to trifle with, for they piled in and I got out of there as fast as the car would take us.

The homes and factories and stores that had bought the gadget were gushing so much dust, visibility wouldn't be worth a damn before long.

I had to wade through about two feet of dust on the laboratory floor to get to Lewis's office and hold a handkerchief over my nose to keep from suffocating.

ALPHA 9

Inside the car we got our faces wiped off and most of the dust hacked out of our throats. I could see then that Lewis was about three shades paler than usual, although to tell the truth, he always was a pasty-looking creature.

"It's the creatures from the third dimension," he said anxiously. "The place where we were sending all the dust. They got sick and tired of having it pour in on them and they got it figured out and now they're firing the dust right back at us."

"Now calm down. We're just jumping at the conclusion that this was caused by our gadget."

"I checked, Joe. It was. The dust is coming out in jets from every single place where we sent it through. No place else."

"Then all we have to do is fire it back at them."

He shook his head. "Not a chance. The gadget works one way now—from them to us." He coughed and looked wildly at me. "Think of it! A couple of million homes, stores, and factories— some of them operating for two whole years! Joe, what are we going to do?"

"We're going to hole up somewhere till this—well, blows over."

Being of a nasty legal turn of mind, he probably foresaw even then the countless lawsuits that would avalanche on us. Personally, I was more scared of being mobbed by angry women.

But that's all past history. We hid out till people had quieted down and then began trying to settle the suits out of court. We had a lot of money and were able to pay off most of them. The judgments against us still outstanding don't amount to more than a few hundred thousand. We could wipe that out pretty quickly if we'd just hit on something else as profitable as the cleaning gadget.

Lewis is working hard at it, but he isn't having any luck. And the Trader is gone now. As soon as we dared come home, I went into the house and had a look at the desk. The inlaid dot was gone. I tried putting something where it had been, but nothing happened.

What scared the Trader off? I'd give a lot to know. Meanwhile, there are some commercial prospects.

The rose-tinted glasses, for instance, that we call the Happiness Lenses. Put them on and you're happy as a clam. Almost every person on the face of the Earth would like a pair of

140

them, so they could forget their troubles for a while. They would probably play hob with the liquor business.

The trouble is that we don't know how to make them and, now that the Trader's gone, we can't swap for them.

But there's one thing that keeps worrying me. I know I shouldn't let it bother me, but I can't keep it out of mind.

Just what did the Trader do with those couple of million zebras we sent him?

GOODLIFE

Fred Saberhagen

Fred Saberhagen is an Illinois-born writer, currently living in the Southwest, whose quiet, sinewy stories have been appearing in print since 1962. Although he has published a number of novels—*The Broken Lands, The Water of Thought, Specimens* — he is best known for the series of short stories he wrote in the mid 1960's about the "Berserkers," colossal planet-sized alien machines of destruction that patrol interstellar space. Though they have been collected in book form (*Berserker*, 1967), a good many of these taut and intense tales have become anthology pieces in their own right, and of them my favorite, I think, is the haunting "Goodlife," second of the series.

If any motion picture company has picked up *Berserker,* I've heard no news of it. Someone in Hollywood is missing a good bet.

I

"It's only a machine, Hemphill," said the dying man in a small voice. Hemphill, drifting weightless in near-darkness, heard him with only faint contempt and pity. Let the wretch go out timidly forgiving the universe everything, if he found the going-out easier that way!

Hemphill kept on staring out through the port, at the dark crenelated shape that blotted out so many of the stars.

There was probably just this one compartment of the passenger ship left livable, with three people on it, and the air whining out in steady leaks that would soon exhaust the emergency tanks. The ship was a wreck, torn and beaten, yet Hemphill's view of the enemy was steady. It must be a force of the enemy's that kept the wreck from spinning.

Now the young woman, another passenger, came drifting across the compartment to touch Hemphill on the arm. He thought her name was Maria something.

"Listen," she began. "Do you think we might—"

In her voice there was no despair, but the tone of planning; and so Hemphill had begun to listen to her. But she was interrupted.

The very walls of the cabin reverberated, driven like speaker diaphragms through the power of the enemy forcefield that still gripped the butchered hull. The voice of the berserker machine came:

"You who can still hear me, live on. I plan to spare you. I am sending a boat to save you from death."

The voice changed tones from word to word, being fragments of the voices of human prisoners the machine had taken and used. It was made of bits of human emotion sorted and fixed, like butterflies on pins. Hemphill was sick with frustrated rage. He had never heard a berserker's voice in reality before, but still it was familiar as an old nightmare. He could feel the woman's hand pull away from his arm, and then he saw that in his rage he had raised both his hands to be claws, then fists that almost smashed themselves against the port. The thing, the damned

thing wanted to take him inside it! Of all people in space it
wanted to make him prisoner!

A plan rose instantly in his mind and flowed smoothly into
action; he spun away from the port. There were warheads, for
small defensive missiles, here in this compartment. He
remembered seeing them.

The other surviving man, a ship's officer, dying slowly,
bleeding through his uniform tatters, saw what Hemphill was
doing in the wreckage, and drifted in front of him interferingly.

"You can't do that... you'll only destroy the boat it
sends... if it lets you do that much... there may be other
people... still alive here..."

The man's face had been upside down before Hemphill as the
two of them drifted. As their movement let them see each other
in normal position, the wounded man stopped talking, gave up
and rotated himself away, drifting inertly as if already dead.

Hemphill could not hope to manage a whole warhead, but he
could extract the chemical-explosive detonator, of a size to carry
under one arm. All passengers had put on emergency spacesuits
when the unequal battle had begun; now he found himself an
extra air tank, and some officer's laser pistol, which he stuck in a
loop of his suit's belt.

The girl approached him again. He watched her warily.

"Do it," she said with quiet conviction, while the three of
them spun slowly in the near-darkness, and the air leaks whined.
"Do it. The loss of a boat will weaken it, a little, for the next
fight. And we here have no chance anyway."

"Yes." He nodded approvingly. This girl understood what
was important: To hurt a berserker, to smash, burn, destroy, to
kill it finally. Nothing else mattered very much.

He pointed to the wounded mate, and whispered: "Don't let
him give me away." She nodded silently. It might hear them
talking. If it could speak through these walls, it could be
listening.

"A boat's coming," said the wounded man, in a calm and
distant voice.

"Goodlife!" called the machine voice cracking between
syllables, as always.

"Here!" He woke up with a start, and got quickly to his feet.

He had been dozing almost under the dripping end of a drinking-water pipe.

"Goodlife!" There were no speakers or scanners in this little compartment; the call came from some distance away.

"Here!" He ran toward the call, his feet shuffling and thumping on metal. He had dozed off, being tired. Even though the battle had been a little one, there had been extra tasks for him, servicing and directing the commensal machines that roamed the endless ducts and corridors repairing damage. It was small help he could give, he knew.

Now his head and neck bore sore spots from the helmet he had had to wear; and his body was chafed in places from the unaccustomed covering he had to put on it when a battle came. This time, happily, there had been no battle damage at all.

He came to the flat glass eye of a scanner, and shuffled to a stop, waiting.

"Goodlife, the perverted machine has been destroyed, and the few badlives left are helpless."

"Yes!" He jiggled his body up and down in happiness.

"I remind you, life is evil," said the voice of the machine.

"Evil is life, I am Goodlife!" he said quickly, ceasing his jiggling. He did not think punishment impended, but he wanted to be sure.

"Yes. Like your parents before you, you have been useful. Now I plan to bring other humans inside myself, to study them closely. Your next use will be with them, in my experiments. I remind you, they are badlife. We must be careful."

"Badlife." He knew they were creatures shaped like himself, existing in the world beyond the machine. They caused the shudders and shocks and damage that made up a battle. "Badlife—here." It was a chilling thought. He raised his own hands and looked at them, then turned his attention up and down the passage in which he stood, trying to visualize the badlife become real before him.

"Go now to the medical room," said the machine. "You must be immunized against disease before you approach the badlife."

Hemphill made his way from one ruined compartment to another, until he found a gash in the outer hull that was plugged nearly shut. While he wrenched on the obstructing material, he heard the clanging arrival of the berserker's boat, come for prisoners. He pulled harder, the obstruction gave, and he was blown out into space.

Around the great wreck were hundreds of pieces of flotsam, held near by tenuous magnetism or perhaps by the berserker's forcefields. Hemphill found that his suit worked well enough. With its tiny jet he moved around the shattered hull to where the boat had come to rest.

The dark blot of the berserker machine came into view against the starfields of deep space, battlemented like a fortified city of old, and far larger than any such city had ever been.

He could see that the berserker's boat had somehow found the right compartment and clamped itself to the wrecked hull. It would be gathering in Maria and the wounded man. Fingers on the plunger that would set off his bomb, Hemphill drifted closer.

On the brink of death, it annoyed him that he would never know with certainty that the boat was destroyed. And it was such a trifling blow to strike, such a small revenge.

Still drifting closer, holding the plunger ready, he saw the puff of decompressed air-moisture as the boat disconnected itself from the hull. The invisible forcefields of the berserker surged, tugging at the boat, at Hemphill, at bits of wreckage within yards of the boat.

He managed to clamp himself to the boat before it was pulled away from him. He thought he had an hour's air in his suit tank, more than he would need.

The berserker pulled him toward itself.

II

The berserkers were relics of some ancient galactic war, some internecine struggle between unheard of races. They were machines set to seek out and destroy life, and each of them bore weapons that could sterilize an Earth-sized planet in two or three days.

Earthmen had spread out among the stars of a little section of an arm of the galactic spiral. Now they reeled back under the emotionless assault of the machines; planets and whole systems were depopulated.

Men fought back when they could. The passenger ship, intercepted far from help, had had no chance; but three or four warships could circle a berserker machine like wolves around a bear, could match missiles and computer speeds with it for long minutes, and—sometimes—could win. For the enemy was old, and damaged by warfare through unknown centuries and systems. Possibly many of them had been destroyed before their swarm descended upon Earthmen. The machines surviving had learned, as machines can learn, to avoid tactical error, and to never forgive the mistakes of an opponent. Their basic built-in order was the destruction of all life encountered. But each machine's strategic schemes were unpredictable, being controlled by the random atomic disintegrations of some longlived radioactive isotope, buried in the center of the mechanism.

Hemphill's mind hung over the brink of death, as his fingers held the plunger of his bomb. The nightcolored enemy was death in his mind; old as a meteorite, a hundred miles or more around its bulging middle. The black scarred surface of it hurtled closer in the unreal starlight, becoming a planet toward which the boat fell.

Hemphill still clung to the boat when it was pulled into an opening that could have accommodated many ships. The size and power of the berserker were all around the man, enough to overwhelm hate and courage alike.

His little bomb was a pointless joke. When the boat touched at a dark internal dock, Hemphill leaped into it and scrambled to find a hiding place.

As he cowered on a shadowed ledge of metal, his hand wanted to fire the bomb, simply to bring death and escape. He forced his hand to be still. He forced himself to watch while the two human prisoners were sucked from the boat through a pulsing transparent tube that passed through a bulkhead. Not knowing what he meant to accomplish, he pushed himself in the direction of the tube. He glided through the dark enormous cavern almost weightlessly; the berserker's mass was enough to give it a small natural gravity of its own.

Within ten minutes he came upon an unmistakable airlock. It seemed to have been cut with a surrounding section of hull from some Earth warship, and set into the bulkhead.

Inside an airlock would be as good a place for a bomb as he

147

was likely to find. He got the outer door open and went in, apparently without triggering any alarms. If he destroyed himself here, he would deprive the berserker of—what? Why should it need an airlock at all?

Not for prisoners, thought Hemphill, if it sucks them in through a tube. Hardly an entrance built for enemies. He tested the air in the lock, and opened his helmet. For airbreathing friends, the size of men? That was a contradiction. Everything that lived and breathed must be a berserker's enemy—except, of course, the unknown beings who had sometimes built it, and loosed it to do what damage it might.

It was thought they were extinct, or unreachably distant in space and time. No defeated and boarded berserker had been found to carry a crew, or to have a place or purpose for a living crew.

|The inner door of the lock opened and artificial gravity came on. Hemphill walked into a narrow and badly lighted passage, his fingers ready on the plunger.

"Go in, Goodlife," said the machine. "Look closely at each of them."

Goodlife made an uncertain sound in his throat, like a servomotor starting and stopping. He was gripped by a feeling resembling hunger, or the fear of punishment— because he was going to see life forms directly now, not as old images on a stage. Knowing the reason for the unpleasant feeling did not help. He stood hesitating outside the door of the room where the badlife was being kept. He had put on his suit again, as the machine had ordered. The suit would protect him if the badlife tried to damage him.

"Go in," the machine repeated.

"Maybe I'd better not," Goodlife said in misery, remembering to speak well and clearly. Punishment was always less likely when he did.

"Punish, punish," said the voice.

When it said the word twice, punishment was very near. As if already feeling in his bones the wrenching pain-that-left-no-damage, he opened the door quickly and stepped in.

He lay on the floor, bloody and damaged, in strange ragged suiting. And at the same time, he was still in the doorway. His own shape was on the floor, the same human form he knew, but now seen entirely from outside. More than an image, far more, it was himself now bi-located. There, here, himself, not himself—

Goodlife fell back against the door. He raised his arm and tried to bite it, forgetting his suit. He pounded his suited arms violently together, until there was bruised pain enough to nail him to himself where he stood.

Slowly, the terror subsided. Gradually his intellect could explain it and master it. This is me, here, here in the doorway. That, *there,* on the floor—that is another life. Another body, corroded like me with vitality. One far worse than I. That one on the floor is badlife.

Maria Juarez had prayed continuously for a long time, her eyes closed. Cold impersonal grippers had moved her this way and that. Her weight had come back, and there was air to breathe when her helmet and her suit had been carefully removed. She opened her eyes and struggled when the grippers began to remove her inner coverall; she saw that she was in a low-ceilinged room, surrounded by man-sized machines of various shapes. When she struggled they paused briefly; then gave up undressing her, chained to the wall by one ankle, and glided away. The dying mate had been dropped at the other end of the room, as if not worth the trouble of further handling.

The man with cold dead eyes, Hemphill, had tried to make a bomb, and failed. Now there would probably be no quick end to life—

When she heard the door operate she opened her eyes again, to watch without comprehension while the bearded young man in the ancient spacesuit went through senseless contortions in the doorway, and finally came forward to stand staring down at the dying man on the floor. The visitor's fingers moved with speed and precision when he raised his hands to the fasteners of his helmet; but the helmet's removal revealed ragged hair and beard framing an idiot's slack face.

He set the helmet down, then scratched and rubbed his hairy head, never taking his eyes from the man on the floor. He had not yet looked once at Maria, and she could look nowhere but at him. She had never seen a face so blank on a living person. This was what happened to a berserker's prisoner!

And yet—and yet Maria had seen the brainwashed, ex-criminals on her own planet. She felt this man was something more—or something less.

The bearded man knelt beside the mate, with an air of hesitation, and reached out to touch him. The dying man stirred feebly, and looked up with comprehension. The floor under him was wet with blood.

The stranger took the mate's limp arm and bent it back and forth, as if interested in the articulation of the human elbow. The mate groaned and struggled feebly. The stranger suddenly shot out his metal-gauntleted hands and seized the dying man by the throat.

Maria could not move or turn her eyes away, though the whole room seemed to spin slowly, then faster and faster, around the focus of those armored hands.

The bearded man released his grip and stood erect, still watching the body at his feet.

"Turned off," he said distinctly.

Perhaps she moved. For whatever reason, the bearded man raised his sleepwalker's face to look at her. He did not meet her eyes, or avoid them. His eye movements were quick and alert, but the muscles of his face just hung there under the skin. He came toward her.

Why, he's young, she thought. Hardly more than a boy. She backed against the wall and waited, standing. Women were not brought up to faint on her planet. Somehow, the closer he came, the less she feared him. But if he had smiled once she would have screamed, on and on.

He stood before her, and reached out one hand to touch her face, her hair, her body. She stood still; she felt no lust in him, no meanness and no kindness. It was as if he radiated an emptiness.

"Not images," said the young man as if to himself. Then another word, sounding like: "Badlife."

Almost Maria dared to speak to him. The strangled man lay on the deck a few yards away.

The young man turned and shuffled deliberately away. She had never seen anyone who walked just like him. He picked up his helmet and went out the door without looking back.

A pipe streamed water into one corner of her little space,

where it gurgled away through a hole in the floor. The gravity seemed to be set at about Earth level. Maria sat leaning against the wall, praying and listening to her heart pound. It almost stopped when the door opened again; only a machine entered, to bring her a large cake of pink and green stuff that seemed to be food. The machine walked around the dead man on its way out.

She had eaten a little of the cake when the door opened again, very slightly at first, then enough for a man to step quickly in. It was Hemphill, the cold-eyed one from the ship, leaning a bit to one side as if dragged down by the weight of the little bomb he still carried under his arm. After a quick look around he shut the door behind him and crossed the room to her, hardly glancing down as he stepped over the body of the mate.

"How many of them are there?" Hemphill whispered, bending over her. She had remained seated on the floor, too surprised to move or speak.

"Who?" she finally managed.

He jerked his head impatiently. "Them. The ones who live here inside *it*, and serve it. I saw one of them coming out of the room, when I was out in the passage. It's fixed up a lot of breathing space for them."

He showed Maria how the bomb could be made to explode, and gave it to her to hold, while he began to burn through her chain with the laser pistol. They exchanged information on what had happened. She did not think she would ever be able to pull the plunger and kill herself, but she did not tell that to Hemphill.

III

Just as they stepped out of the prison room, Hemphill had a bad moment when three machines rolled toward them from around a corner. But the things ignored the two frozen humans and rolled silently past them, going on out of sight.

He turned to Maria with an exultant whisper: "The damned thing is three-quarters blind, here inside its own skin!"

She only waited, watching him with frightened eyes.

With the beginning of hope, a vague plan was forming in his mind. He led her on, saying: "Now we'll see about that man. Or men." Was it too good to be true, that there was only one of them?

The corridors were badly lit, with uneven jogs and steps in them. Carelessly built concessions to life, he thought. He moved in the direction he had seen the man take.

After a few minutes of cautious advance, Hemphill heard the shuffling footsteps of one person ahead, coming nearer. He handed the bomb to Maria again, and pressed her behind him. They waited in a dark niche.

The footsteps approached with careless speed, a vague shadow bobbing ahead of them. The shaggy head swung so abruptly into view that Hemphill's metal-fisted swing was almost too late. The blow only grazed the back of the skull; the man yelped and staggered off balance and fell down. He was wearing an old-model spacesuit, with no helmet.

Hemphill crouched over him, shoving the laser pistol almost into his face. "Make a sound and I'll kill you. Where are the others?"

The face looking up at Hemphill was stunned—worse than stunned. It seemed more dead than alive, though the eyes moved alertly enough from Hemphill to Maria and back, disregarding the gun.

"He's the same one," Maria whispered.

The man felt the back of his head, where he had been hit. "Damage," he said tonelessly, as if to himself. Then he reached up for the pistol, so calmly and steadily that he was nearly able to touch it.

Hemphill jumped back a step, and barely kept himself from firing. "Sit still or I'll kill you! Now tell me who you are, and how many others are here."

The man's putty face showed nothing. He said: "Your speech is steady in tone from word to word, not like that of the machine. You hold a killing tool there. Give it to me, and I will destroy you and—that one."

It seemed this man was only a brainwashed ruin, instead of an unspeakable traitor. Now what use could be made of him? Hemphill moved back another step, slowly lowering the pistol.

Maria spoke to their prisoner. "Where are you from? What planet?"

A blank stare.

She repeated the question in a couple of other languages, with no better result, then returned to the universal Loglan of Earth's spacemen and colonists.

"Your home. Where were you born?"

"From the birth tank." Sometimes the tones of the man's voice shifted like the berserker's, as if he were a fearful comedian mocking it.

Hemphill gave an unstable laugh. "From a birth tank, of course. What else? Where are the others?"

"I do not understand."

Hemphill sighed. "All right. Where's this birth tank?"

The place looked like the storeroom of a biology lab, badly lighted, with equipment piled and crowded, laced with pipes and conduits. But perhaps no living technician had ever worked here.

"You were *born* here?" Hemphill demanded.

"Yes."

"He's crazy."

"No, wait." Maria's voice sank to an even lower whisper, as if she was frightened anew. She took the hand of the slack-faced man, and he bent his head to stare at their touching hands.

"Do you have a name?" she asked, as if of a lost child.

"I am Goodlife."

"I think it's hopeless," put in Hemphill

The girl ignored him. "Goodlife? My name is Maria. And this is Hemphill."

No reaction.

"Who were your parents? Father? Mother?"

"They were goodlife too. They helped the machine. There was a battle, and badlife killed them. But they had given cells of their bodies to the machine, and from them it made me. Now I am the only goodlife."

"Great God," whispered Hemphill.

Silent, awed attention seemed to move Goodlife when threats and pleas had not. His face moved in awkward grimaces; then he turned to stare into a corner. For almost the first time, he volunteered a communication: "I know they were like you. A man and a woman."

Hemphill wanted to sweep every cubic foot of the miles of mechanism with his hatred; he looked around.

"The damned things," he said, his voice cracking like the berserker's own. "What they've done to me. To you. To everyone."

Plans seemed to come when the strain of hating was greatest. He moved quickly to put a hand on Goodlife's shoulder. "Listen to me. Do you know what a radioactive isotope is?"

"Yes."

"There will be a place, somewhere, where the —the machine decides what it will do next—what strategy to follow. A place holding a block of some isotope with a long half-life. Probably near the center of the machine. Do you know of such a place?"

"Yes, I know where the strategic housing is."

"Strategic housing." Hope mounted to a strong new level. "Is there a way for us to reach it?"

"You are badlife!" He knocked Hemphill's hand away, awkwardly. "You want to damage the machine, and you have damaged me. You are to be destroyed."

Maria took over, trying to soothe. "Goodlife—we are not bad, this man and I. Those who built this machine are the badlife. Someone built it, you know, some living people built it, long ago. They were the real badlife."

"Badlife." He might be agreeing with Maria, or accusing her.

"Don't you want to live, Goodlife? Hemphill and I want to live. We want to help you, because you're alive, like us. Won't you help us now?"

Goodlife was silent for a few moments. Then he turned back to face them and said: "All life thinks it is, but it is not. There are only particles, energy, and space, and the laws of the machines."

Maria kept at him. "Goodlife, listen to me. A wise man one said: 'I think, therefore I am.'"

"A wise man?" he questioned, in his cracking voice. Then he sat down on the deck, hugging his knees and rocking back and forth. He might be thinking.

Drawing Maria aside, Hemphill said: "You know, we have a faint hope now. There's plenty of air in here, there's water and food. There are warships following this thing, there must be. If we can find a way to disable it, we can wait and maybe be picked up in a month or two."

She watched him silently for a moment. "Hemphill—what have these machines done to you?"

"My wife—my children." He thought his voice sounded

almost indifferent. "They were on Pascalo, three years ago; there was nothing left. This machine, or one like it."

She took his hand, as she had taken Goodlife's. They both looked down at the joined fingers, then raised their eyes, smiling briefly together at the similarity of action.

"Where's the bomb?" Hemphill thought aloud suddenly, spinning around.

It lay in a dim corner. He grabbed it up again, and strode over to where Goodlife sat and rocked.

"Well, are you with us? Us, or the ones who built the machine?"

Goodlife stood up, and looked closely at Hemphill. "They were inspired by the laws of physics, which controlled their brains, to build the machine. Now the machine has preserved them as images. It has preserved my father and mother, and it will preserve me."

"The images do you mean? Where are they?"

"The images in the theater."

The right course seemed to be to accustom him to cooperation, win his confidence, learn about him and the machine. Then, to the strategic housing.

"Will you guide us to the theater, Goodlife?"

It was by far the largest airfilled room they had yet found, with a hundred seats of a shape usable by Earthmen, though Hemphill guessed it had been built for someone else. The theater was elaborately furnished and well lighted. When the door closed behind them, the ranked images of intelligent creatures brightened into life upon the stage.

The stage became a window into a vast hall. One person stood forward at an imaged lectern; he was a slender, fine-boned being, topologically like a man except for the single eye that stretched across his face, with a bright bulging pupil that slid to and fro like mercury.

The speaker's voice was a high-pitched torrent of clicks and whines. Most of those in the ranks behind him wore a kind of uniform. When he paused, they whined in unison.

"What does he say?" Maria whispered.

Goodlife looked at her. "The machine has told me that it has lost the meaning of the sounds."

"Then may we see the images of your parents, Goodlife?"

Hemphill, watching the stage, started to object; but the girl was right. The sight of this fellow's parents might be more immediately helpful.

Goodlife found a control somewhere.

Hemphill was surprised momentarily that the parents appeared only in flat projected pictures. First the man was there, against a plain background, blue eyes and neat short beard, nodding his head with a pleasant expression on his face. He wore the lining coverall of a spacesuit.

Then the woman, holding some kind of cloth before her for covering, and looking straight into the camera. She had a broad face and red braided hair. There was hardly time to see anything more before the alien orator was back, whining faster than ever.

Hemphill turned to ask: "Is that all? All you know of your parents?"

"Yes. Now they are images, they no longer think they exist. The badlife killed them."

The creature in the projection was assuming, Maria thought, a more didactic tone. Three-dimensional charts of stars and planets appeared near him, one after another, and he gestured at them as he spoke. He had vast numbers of stars and planets on his charts to boast about; she could tell somehow that he was boasting.

Hemphill was moving toward the stage a step at a time, more and more absorbed. Maria did not like the way the light of the images reflected on his face.

Goodlife, too, watched the stage pageant which perhaps he had seen a thousand times before. Maria could not tell what thoughts might be behind his meaningless face which had never had another human face to imitate. On impulse she took his arm again.

"Goodlife, Hemphill and I are alive, like you. Will you help us now? Then we will always help you." She had a sudden mental picture of Goodlife rescued, taken to a planet, cowering among the staring badlife

"Good. Bad." His hand reached to take hold of hers; he had removed his suit gauntlets. He swayed back and forth as if she attracted and repelled him at the same time. God, she wanted to scream and wail for him, to tear apart with her fingers the mindlessly proceeding metal that had made him what he was.

"We've got them!" It was Hemphill, coming back from the stage, where the recorded tirade went on unrelentingly. He was exultant. "Don't you see? He's showing what must be a complete catalogue, of every star and rock they own. It's a victory speech. But when we study those charts we can find them, we can track them down and *reach* them!"

"Hemphill." She wanted to calm him back to concentration on immediate problems. "How old are those—pictures, up there? What part of the galaxy do they show? Or were they even made in another galaxy? Will we ever be able to tell?"

Hemphill lost some enthusiasm. "Anyway, it's a chance to track them down; we've got to save this information." He pointed at Goodlife. "He's got to take me to what he calls the strategic housing; then we can sit and wait for the warships, or maybe get off this damned thing in a boat."

She stroked Goodlife's hand, soothing a baby. "Yes, but he's confused. How could he be anything else?"

"Of course." Hemphill paused to consider. "You can handle him much better than I."

She didn't answer.

Hemphill went on: "Now you're a woman, and he appears to be a physically healthy young male. Calm him down if you like, but somehow you've *got* to persuade him to help me. Everything depends on it." He had turned toward the stage again, unable to keep half his mind from the star charts. "Take him out somewhere, for a little walk and talk; don't get far away."

And what else was there to do? She led Goodlife from the theater while the dead man on the stage clicked and shouted, cataloguing his thousand suns.

IV

Too much had happened, was still happening, and all at once he could no longer stand to be near the badlife. Goodlife found himself pulling away from the female, running, flying down the passages, toward the place where he had fled when he was small and strange fears had come from nowhere. It was the room where the machine always saw and heard him, and was ready to talk to him.

He stood before the attention of the machine, in the chamber-that-has-shrunk. He thought of the place so, because he could remember it clearly as a larger room, where the scanners and speakers of the machine towered above his head. He knew the real change had been his own physical growth; still, this compartment was set apart in a special association with food and sleep and protective warmth.

"I have listened to the badlife, and shown them things," he said, fearing punishment.

"I know that, Goodlife, for I have watched. These things have become a part of my experiment."

What joyous relief! It said nothing of punishment, though it must know that the words of the badlife had shaken and confused him. He had even imagined himself showing the man Hemphill the strategic housing, and so putting an end to all punishment; for always.

"They wanted me—they wanted me to—"

"I have watched. I have listened. The man is tough and evil, powerfully motivated to fight against me. I must understand his kind, for they cause much damage. He must be tested to his limits, to destruction. He thinks himself free inside me, and so he will not think as a prisoner. This is important."

Goodlife pulled off his irritating suit; the machine would not let the badlife in here. He sank down to the floor and wrapped his arms around the base of a scanner-speaker console. Once long ago the machine had given him a thing that was soft and warm when he held it... he closed his eyes.

"What are my orders?" he asked, sleepily. Here in this chamber all was steady and comforting, as always.

"First, do not tell the badlife of these orders. Then, do what the man Hemphill tells you to do. No harm will come to me."

"I watched his approach, and I disabled his bomb, even before he entered to attack me. His pistol can do me no serious harm. Do you think one badlife can conquer me?"

"No." Smiling, reassured, he curled into a more comfortable position. "Tell me about my parents." He had heard the story a thousand times, but it was always good.

"Your parents were good, they gave themselves to me. Then,

during a great battle, the badlife killed them. The badlife hated them, as they hate you. When they say they like you, they lie, with the evil untruth of all badlife.

"But your parents had each given me a part of their bodies, and from them I made you. Your parents were destroyed completely by the badlife, or I would have saved even their non-functioning bodies for you to see. That would have been good."

"Yes."

"The two badlives have searched for you; now they are resting. Sleep, Goodlife."

He slept.

Awakening, he remembered a dream in which two people had beckoned him to join them on the stage of the theater. He knew they were his mother and father, though they looked like the two badlife. The dream faded before his waking mind could grasp it firmly.

He ate and drank, while the machine talked to him.

"If the man Hemphill wants to be guided to the strategic housing, take him there. I will capture him there, and let him escape later to try again. When finally he can be provoked to fight no more, I will destroy him. But I mean to preserve the life of the female; you and she will produce more goodlife for me "

"Yes!" It was immediately clear what a good thing that would be. They would give parts of their bodies to the machine, so new goodlife bodies could be built, cell by cell. And the man Hemphill, who punished and damaged with his fast-swinging arm, would be utterly destroyed.

When he rejoined the badlife, the man Hemphill barked questions and threatened punishment until Goodlife was confused and a little frightened. But Goodlife agreed to help, and was careful to reveal nothing of what the machine planned. Maria was more pleasant than ever. He touched her whenever he could.

Hemphill demanded to be taken to the strategic housing. Goodlife agreed at once; he had been there many times. There was a high-speed elevator that made the fifty-mile journey easy.

Hemphill paused, before saying: "You're too damn willing all of a sudden." Turning his face to Maria. "I don't trust him."

This badlife thought he was being false! Goodlife was

angered; the machine never lied, and no properly obedient goodlife could lie.

Hemphill paced around, and finally demanded: "Is there any route that approaches this strategic housing in such a way that the machine cannot possibly watch us?"

Goodlife thought. "I believe there is one such way. We will have to carry extra tanks of air, and travel many miles through vacuum." The machine had said to help Hemphill, and help he would. He hoped he could watch when the male badlife was finally destroyed.

There had been a battle, in some time that could hardly be related meaningfully to any Earthly calendar. The berserker had fought some terrible opponent, and had taken a terrible lance-thrust of a wound. A cavity two miles wide at the widest, and fifty miles deep, had been driven in by a sequence of shaped atomic charges, through level after level of machinery, deck after deck of armor, and had been stopped only by the last inner defenses of the buried unliving heart. The berserker had survived, and crushed its enemy, and soon afterward its repair machines had sealed over the outer opening of the wound, using extra thicknesses of armor. It had meant to gradually rebuild the whole destruction; but there was so much life in the galaxy, and so much of it was stubborn and clever. Somehow battle damage accumulated faster than it could be repaired. The great hole was used as a conveyor path, and never much worked on.

When Hemphill saw the blasted cavity—what little of it his tiny suit-lamp could show—he felt a shrinking fear that was greater than any in his memory. He stopped on the edge of the void, drifting there with his arm instinctively around Maria. She had put on a suit and accompanied him, without protest or eagerness, without being asked.

It had already been an hour's journey from the airlock, through weightless vacuum inside the great machine. Goodlife had led the way through section after section, with every show of cooperation. Hemphill had the pistol ready, and the bomb, and two hundred feet of cord tied around his left arm.

But when Hemphill recognized the once-molten edge of the berserker's great scar for what it was, his delicate new hope of survival left him. This, the damned thing had survived. This, perhaps, had hardly weakened it. Again, the bomb under his arm was only a pathetic toy.

Goodlife drifted up to them. Hemphill had already taught him to touch helmets for speech in vacuum.

"This great damage is the one path we can take to reach the strategic housing without passing scanners or service machines. I will teach you to ride the conveyor. It will carry us most of the way."

The conveyor was a thing of forcefields and great rushing containers, hundreds of yards out in the Great Damage and running lengthwise through it. When the conveyor's forcefields caught the people up, their weightlessness was more than ever like falling, with occasional vast shapes, corpuscles of the berserker's bloodstream, flickering past in the near-darkness to show movement.

Hemphill flew beside Maria, holding her hand. Her face was hard to see inside the helmet, but she did not seem to be looking at him. There was no need.

This conveyor was another mad new world, a fairy tale of monsters and flying and falling. Hamphill fell past his great fear, into a calm determination.

I can do it, he thought. The thing is blind and helpless here. I will do it, and I will survive if I can.

Goodlife led them from the slowing conveyor, to drift into a chamber hollowed in the inner armor by the final explosion at the end of the ancient lance-thrust. The chamber was an empty sphere a hundred feet across, from which cracks radiated out into the solid armor. On the surface nearest the center of the berserker, one fissure was as wide as a door, where the last energy of the enemy's blow had driven ahead.

Goodlife touched helmets. "I have seen the other end of this crack, from inside, at the strategic housing. It is only a few yards from here." Hemphill hesitated for only a moment, wondering whether to send Goodlife through the twisting passage first. But if this was some incredibly complex trap, the trigger of it might be anywhere.

He touched his helmet to Maria's. "Stay behind him. Follow him through, and keep an eye on him."

The fissure narrowed as Hemphill followed it, but at the end it was still wide enough for him to force himself through.

ALPHA 9

This was the inner temple, and another great hollow sphere. In the center was a complexity the size of a small house, shock-mounted on a web of girders that ran in every direction. This could be nothing but the strategic housing. There was a glow from it like flickering moonlight; forcefield switches responding to the random atomic turmoil within, somehow choosing what human shipping lane or colony would be next attacked, and how.

Hemphill felt a pressure rising in his mind and soul, toward a climax of triumphal hate. He drifted forward, cradling his bomb tenderly, starting to unwind the cord wrapped around his arm. He tied the free end delicately to the plunger of the bomb, as he approached the central complex.

I mean to live, he thought, to watch the damned thing die. I will tape the bomb against the central block, that so-innocent looking slab in there, and I will brace myself around two hundred feet of these heavy metal corners, and pull.

Goodlife stood braced in the perfect place from which to watch the heart of the machine, watching the man Hemphill string his cord. Goodlife felt a certain satisfaction that his prediction had been right and that the strategic housing was approachable by this one narrow path of the great damage. They would not have to go back that way. When the badlife had been captured, all of them could ride up in the air-filled elevator Goodlife used when he came here for maintenance practice.

Hemphill had finished stringing his cord. Now he waved his arm at Goodlife and Maria, who clung to the same girder, watching. Now Hemphill pulled on the cord. Of course, nothing happened. The machine had said the bomb was disabled, and the machine would make very certain in such a matter.

Maria pushed away from beside Goodlife, and drifted in toward Hemphill.

Hemphill tugged again and again on his cord. Goodlife sighed impatiently, and moved. There was a great cold in the girders here; he could begin to feel it now through the fingers and toes of his suit.

At last, when Hemphill started back to see what was wrong with his device, the service machines came from where they had

162

been hiding, to seize him. He tried to draw his pistol, but their grippers moved far too quickly.

It was hardly a struggle that Goodlife saw, but he watched with interest. Hemphill's figure had gone rigid in the suit, obviously straining every muscle to the limit. Why should the badlife try to struggle against steel and atomic power? The machines bore the man effortlessly away, toward the elevator shaft. Goodlife felt an uneasiness.

Maria was drifting, her face turned back toward Goodlife. He wanted to go to her and touch her again, but suddenly he was a little afraid, as before when he had run from her. One of the service machines came back from the elevator to grip her and carry her away. She kept her face turned toward Goodlife. He turned away from her, a feeling like punishment in the core of his being.

In the great cold silence, the flickering light from the strategic housing bathed everything. In the center, a chaotic block of atoms. Elsewhere, engines, relays, sensing cells. Where was it, really, the great machine that spoke to him? Everywhere, and nowhere. Would these new feelings, brought by the badlife, ever leave him? He tried to understand himself, and could not begin.

Light flickered on a round shape among the girders and a few yards away, a shape that offended Goodlife's sense of the proper and necessary in machinery, Looking closer, he saw that it was a space helmet.

The motionless figure was wedged only lightly in an angle between frigid beams, but there was no force in here to move it.

He could hear the suit creak, stiff with great cold, when he grabbed it and turned it. Unseeing blue eyes looked out at Goodlife through the faceplate. The man's face wore a neat short beard.

"Ahhh, yes," sighed Goodlife inside his own helmet. A thousand times he had seen this face.

His father had been carrying something, heavy, strapped carefully to his ancient suit. His father had carried it this far, until the old suit had wheezed and failed.

His father, too, had followed the logical narrow path of the great damage, to reach the strategic housing without being seen. His father had choked and died and frozen here, carrying toward strategic housing what could only be a bomb.

Goodlife heard his own voice keening, without words, and he could not see plainly for the tears floating in his helmet. His fingers felt numbed with cold as he unstrapped the bomb and lifted it from his father...

V

Hemphill was too exhausted to do more than gasp as the service machine carried him out of the elevator and along the air-filled corridor toward the prison room. When the machine went dead and dropped him, he had to lie still for long seconds before he could attack it again. It had hidden his pistol somewhere, so he began to beat on the robotlike thing with his armored fists, while it stood unresisting. Soon it toppled over. Hemphill sat on it and beat it some more, sobbing.

It was nearly a minute later when the tremor of the explosion, racing from the compounded chaos of the berserker's torn-out heart, racing through metal beams and decks, reached the corridor, where it was far too faint for anyone to feel.

Maria, completely weary, sat where her metal captor had dropped her, watching Hemphill, pitying him and loving him.

He stopped his pointless pounding of the machine under him, and said hoarsely: "It's a trick, another damned trick."

The tremor had been too faint for anyone to feel, here, but Maria shook her head. "No, I don't think so." She saw that power still seemed to be on the elevator, and she watched the door of it.

Hemphill went away to search among the now-purposeless machines for weapons and food. He came back, raging again. What was probably an automatic destructor charge had wrecked the theater and the star charts. They might as well get away in the boat.

She ignored him, still watching an elevator door which never opened. Soon she began quietly to cry.

NOBODY'S HOME

Joanna Russ

Now and again a science-fiction story comes along that conveys, in an inescapably plausible way, a quality of what it will really be like to live in some corner of the future. Fritz Leiber did it in "Coming Attraction," Robert A. Heinlein in "The Roads Must Roll," Frederik Pohl in "Day Million"—none of them stories of spaceships and galactic empires and cosmic warfare, all of them providing a striking and unforgettable glimpse of tomorrow or the day after tomorrow. To which we can add this sleek and glistening vision of the family of the future by Joanna Russ, author of *Picnic on Paradise, And Chaos Died, The Female Man,* and assorted other ferociously inventive stories.

After she had finished her work at the North Pole, Jannina came down to the Red Sea refineries, where she had family business, jumped to New Delhi for dinner, took a nap in a public hotel in Queensland, walked from the hotel to the station, bypassed the Leeward Islands (where she thought she might go, but all the stations were busy), and met Charley to watch the dawn of the Carolinas.

"Where've you *been,* dear C?"

"Tanzania. And you're married."

"No."

"I heard you were married," he said. "The Lees told the Smiths who told the Kerguelens who told the Utsumbés and we get around, we Utsumbés. A new wife, they said. I didn't know you were especially fond of women."

"I'm not. She's my husbands' wife. And we're not married yet, Charley. She's had hard luck: a first family started in '35, two husbands burned out by an overload while arranging transportation for a concert—of all things, pushing papers, you know!—and the second divorced her, I think, and she drifted away from the third (a big one), and there was some awful quarrel with the fourth, people chasing people around tables, I don't know."

"Poor woman."

In the manner of people joking and talking lightly they had drawn together, back to back, sitting on the ground and rubbing together their shoulders and the backs of their heads. Jannina said sorrowfully, "What lovely hair you have, Charley Utsumbé, like metal mesh."

"All we Utsumbés are exceedingly handsome." They linked arms. The sun, which anyone could chase around the world now, see it rise or set twenty times a day, fifty times a day—if you wanted to spend your life like that—rose dripping out of the cypress swamp. There was nobody around for miles. Mist drifted up from the pools and low places.

"My God," he said, "it's summer! I have to be at Tanga now."

"What?" said Jannina.

"One loses track," he said apologetically. "I'm sorry, love, but I have unavoidable business at home. Tax labor."

"But why summer, why did its being summer—"

"Train of thought! Too complicated" (and already they were out of key, already the mild affair was over, there having come between them the one obligation that can't be put off to the time you like, or the place you like; off he'd go to plug himself into a road-member or a doctor, though it's of some advantage to mend all the roads of a continent at one time).

She sat cross-legged on the station platform, watching him enter the booth and set the dial. He stuck his head out the glass door.

"Come with me to Africa, lovely lady!"

She thumbed her nose at him. "You're only a passing fancy, Charley U!" He blew a kiss, enclosed himself in the booth, and disappeared. (The transmatter field is larger than the booth, for obvious reasons; the booth flicks on and off several million times a second and so does not get transported itself, but it protects the machinery from the weather and it keeps people from losing elbows or knees or slicing the ends off a package or a child. The booths at the cryogenics center at the North Pole have exchanged air so often with those of warmer regions that each has its own microclimate; leaves and seeds, plants and earth are piled about them. Don't Step on the Grass!—say the notes pinned to the door—Wish to Trade Pawlownia Sapling for Sub-arctic Canadian Moss; Watch Your Goddamn Bare Six-Toed Feet!; Wish Amateur Cellist for Quartet, Six Months' Rehearsal! Late Uhl with Reciter; I Lost a Squirrel Here Yesterday, Can You Find It Before It Dies? Eight Children Will Be Heartbroken—Cecila Ching, Buenos Aires.)

Jannina sighed and slipped on her glass woolly; nasty to get back into clothes, but home was cold. You never knew where you might go, so you carried them. Years ago (she thought) I came here with someone in the dead of winter, either an unmatched man or someone's starting spouse—only two of us, at any rate—and we waded through the freezing water and danced as hard as we could and then proved we could sing and drink beer in a swamp at the same time. Good Lord! And then went to the public resort on the Ile de la Cité to watch professional plays, opera, games—you have to be good to get in there!—and got into some clothes because it was chilly after sundown in September—no wait, it was Venezuela—and watched the lights come out and smoked like mad at a café table and tickled the robot waiter and pretended we were old, really old, perhaps a hundred and fifty.... Years ago!

But *was* it the same place? she thought, and dismissing the incident forever, she stepped into the booth, shut the door, and dialed home: the Himalayas. The trunk line was clear. The branch stop was clear. The family's transceiver (located in the anteroom behind two doors, to keep the task of heating the house within reasonable limits) had damn well better be clear, or somebody would be blown right into the vestibule. Momentum- and heat-compensators kept Jannina from arriving home at seventy degrees Fahrenheit internal temperature (seven degrees lost for every mile you teleport upward) or too many feet above herself (rise to the east, drop going west, to the north or south you are apt to be thrown right through the wall of the booth). Someday (thought Jannina) everybody will decide to let everybody live in decent climates. But not yet. Not this everybody.

She arrived home singing "The World's My Back Yard, Yes, the World Is My Oyster," a song that had been popular in her first youth, some seventy years before.

The Komarovs' house was hardened foam with an automatic inside line to the school near Naples. It was good to be brought up on your own feet. Jannina passed through; the seven-year-olds lay with their heads together and their bodies radiating in a six-personed asterisk. In this position (which was supposed to promote mystical thought) they played Barufaldi; guessing the identity of famous dead personages through anagrammatic sentences, the first letters of the words of which (unscrambled into aphorisms or proverbs) simultaneously spelled out a moral and a series of Goedel numbers (in a previously agreed-upon code) which—

"Oh, my darling, how felicitous is the advent of your appearance!" cried a boy (hard to take, the polysyllabic stage). "Embrace me, dearest maternal parent! Unite your valuable upper limbs about my eager person!"

"Vulgar!" said Jannina, laughing.

"Non sum filius tuus?" said the child.

"No, you're not my body-child; you're my godchild. Your mother bequeathed me to you when she died. What are you learning?"

"The eternal parental question," he said, frowning. "How to run a helicopter. How to prepare food from its actual, revolting, raw constituents. Can I go now?"

"*Can* you?" she said. "Nasty imp!"

"Good," he said. "I've made you feel guilty. Don't *do* that," and as she tried to embrace him, he ticklishly slid away. "The robin walks quietly up the branch of the tree," he said breathlessly, flopping back on the floor.

"That's not an aphorism." (Another Barafuldi player.)

"It is."

"It isn't."

"It is."

"It isn't."

"It is."

"It—"

The school vanished; the antechamber appeared. In the kitchen Chi Komarov was rubbing the naked back of his sixteen-year-old son. Parents always kissed each other; children always kissed each other. She touched foreheads with the two men and hung her woolly on the hook by the ham radio rig. Someone was always around. Jannina flipped the cover off her wrist chronometer; standard regional time, date, latitude-longitude, family computer hookup clear. "At my age I ought to remember these things," she said. She pressed the computer hookup: Ann at tax labor in the schools, bit-a-month plan, regular Ann; Lee with three months to go, five years off, heroic Lee; Phuong in Paris, still rehearsing; C.E. gone, won't say where, spontaneous C.E.; Ilse making some repairs in the basement, not a true basement, really, but the room farthest down the hillside. She went up the stairs and then came down and put her head round at the living-and-swimming room. Through the glass wall one could see the mountains. Old Al who had joined them late in life, did a bit of gardening in the brief summers, and generally stuck around the place. Jannina beamed. "Hullo, Old Al!" Big and shaggy, a rare delight, his white body hair. She sat on his lap. "Has she come?"

"The new one? No," he said.

"Shall we go swimming?"

He made an expressive face. "No, dear," he said. "I'd rather go to Naples and watch the children fly helicopters. I'd rather go to Nevada and fly them myself. I've been in the water all day, watching a very dull person restructure coral reefs and experiment with polyploid polyps."

"You mean *you* were doing it."

"One gets into the habit of working."

"But you didn't have to!"

"It was a private project. Most interesting things are."

She whispered in his ear.

With happily flushed faces, they went into Old Al's inner garden and locked the door.

Jannina, temporary family representative, threw the computer helmet over her head and, thus plugged in, she cleaned house, checked food supplies, did a little of the legal business entailed by a family of eighteen adults (two triplet marriages, a quad, and group of eight). She felt very smug. She put herself through by radio to Himalayan HQ (above two thousand meters) and hooking computer to computer—a very odd feeling, like an urge to sneeze that never comes off—extended a formal invitation to one Leslie Smith ("Come stay, why don't you?"), notifying every free Komarov to hop it back and fast. Six hikers might come for the night—back packers. More food. First thunderstorm of the year in Albany, New York (North America). Need an extra two rooms by Thursday. Hear the Palnatoki are moving. Can't use a room. Can't use a kitten. Need the geraniums back, Mrs. Adam, Chile. The best maker of hand-blown glass in the world has killed in a duel the second-best maker of hand-blown glass for joining the movement toward ceramics. A bitter struggle is foreseen in the global economy. Need a lighting designer. Need fifteen singers and electric pansensicon. Standby tax labor xxxxxpj through xxxyq to Cambalue, great tectogenic—

With the guilty feeling that one always gets gossiping with a computer, for it's really not reciprocal, Jannina flipped off the helmet. She went to get Ilse. Climbing back through the white foam room, the purple foam room, the green foam room, everything littered with plots and projects of the clever Komarovs or the even cleverer Komarov children, stopping at the baby room for Ilse to nurse her baby. Jannina danced staidly around studious Ilse. They turned on the nursery robot and the television screen. Ilse drank beer in the swimming room, for her milk. She worried her way through the day's record of events—faults in the foundation, some people who came from Chichester and couldn't find C.E. so one of them burst into tears, a new

170

experiment in genetics coming round the gossip circuit, an execrable set of equations from some imposter in Bucharest.

"A duel!" said Jannina.

They both agreed it was shocking. And what fun. A new fashion. You had to be a little mad to do it. Awful.

The light went on over the door to the tunnel that linked the house to the antechamber, and very quickly, one after another, as if the branch line had just come free, eight Komarovs came into the room. The light flashed again; one could see three people debouch one after the other, persons in boots, with coats, packs, and face masks over their woollies. They were covered with snow, either from the mountain terraces above the house or from some other place, Jannina didn't know. They stamped the snow off in the antechamber and hung their clothes outside; "Good heavens, you're not circumcised!" cried someone. There was much handshaking and embracing all around as at a wedding party. Velet Komarov (the short, dark one) recognized Fung Pao-yu and swung her off her feet. People began to joke, tentatively stroking one another's arms. "Did you have a good hike? Are you a good hiker, Pao-yu?" said Velet. The light over the antechamber went on again, though nobody could see a thing since the glass was steamed over from the collision of hot with cold air. Old Al stopped, halfway into the kitchen. The baggage receipt chimed, recognized only by family ears—upstairs a bundle of somebody's things, ornaments, probably, for the missing Komarovs were still young and the young are interested in clothing, were appearing in the baggage receptacle. "Ann or Phuong?" said Jannina. "Five to three, anybody? Match me!" but someone strange opened the door of the booth and peered out. Oh, a dizzying sensation. She was painted in a few places, which was awfully odd because really it was old-fashioned; and why do it for a family evening? It was a stocky young woman. It was an awful mistake (though Jannina). Then the visitor made her second mistake. She said:

"I'm Leslie Smith." But it was more through clumsiness than being rude. Chi Komarov (the tall, blond one) saw this instantly and, snatching off his old-fashioned spectacles, he ran to her side and patted her, saying teasingly:

"Now, haven't we met? Now, aren't you married to someone I know?"

"No, no," said Leslie Smith, flushing with pleasure.

He touched her neck. "Ah, you're a tightrope dancer!"

"Oh, no!" exclaimed Leslie Smith.

"*I'm* a tightrope dancer," said Chi. "Would you believe it?"

"But you're too—too *spiritual*," said Leslie Smith hesitantly.

"Spiritual, how do you like that, family, spiritual?" he cried, delighted (a little more delighted, thought Jannina, than the situation really called for) and he began to stroke her neck.

"What a lovely neck you have," he said.

This steadied Leslie Smith. She said, "I like tall men," and allowed herself to look at the rest of the family. "Who are these people?" she said, though one was afraid she might really mean it.

Fung Pao-yu to the rescue: "Who are these people? Who are they, indeed! I doubt if they are anybody. One might say, 'I have met these people,' but has one? What existential meaning would such a statement convey? I myself, now, I have met them. I have been introduced to them. But they are like the Sahara; it is all wrapped in mystery; I doubt if they even have names," etc. etc. Then lanky Chi Komarov disputed possession of Leslie Smith with Fung Pao-yu, and Fung Pao-yu grabbed one arm and Chi the other; and she jumped up and down fiercely; so that by the time the lights dimmed and the food came, people were feeling better—or so Jannina judged. So embarrassing and delightful to be eating fifteen to a room! "We Komarovs are famous for eating whatever we can get whenever we can get it," said Velet proudly. Various Komarovs in various places, with the three hikers on cushions and Ilse at full length on the rug. Jannina pushed a button with her toe and the fairy lights came on all over the ceiling. "The children did that," said Old Al. He had somehow settled at Leslie Smith's side and was feeding her so-chi from his own bowl. She smiled up at him "We once," said a hiking companion of Fung Pao-yu's, "arranged a dinner in an amphitheater where half of us played servants to the other half, with forfeits for those who didn't show. It was the result of a bet. Like the bad old days. Did you know there were once *five billion people* in this world?"

"The gulls," said Ilse, "are mating on the Isle of Skye." There were murmurs of appreciative interest. Chi began to develop an erection and everyone laughed. Old Al wanted music and Velet didn't; what might have been a quarrel was ended by Ilse's furiously boxing their ears. She stalked off to the nursery.

"Leslie Smith and I are both old-fashioned," said Old Al, "because neither of us believes in gabbing. Chi—your theater?"

"We're turning people away." He leaned forward, earnestly, tapping his fingers on his crossed knees. "I swear, some of them are threatening to commit suicide."

"It's a choice," said Velet reasonably.

Leslie Smith had dropped her bowl. They retrieved it for her.

"Aiy, I remember—" said Pao-yu. "What I remember! We've been eating dried mush for three days, tax-issue. Did you know one of my dads killed himself?"

"No!" said Velet, surprised.

"Years ago," said Pao-yu. "He said he refused to live to see the time when chairs were reintroduced. He also wanted further genetic engineering, I believe, for even more intelligence. He did it out of spite, I'm sure. I think he wrestled a shark. Jannina, is this tax-issue food? Is it this year's style tax-issue sauce?"

"No, next year's," said Jannina snappishly. Really, some people! She slipped into Finnish, to show up Pao-yu's pronunciation. "Isn't that so?" she asked Leslie Smith.

Leslie Smith stared at her.

More charitably Jannina informed them all, in Finnish, that the Komarovs had withdrawn their membership in a food group, except for Ann, who had taken out an individual, because what the dickens, who had the time? And tax-issue won't kill you. As they finished, they dropped their dishes into the garbage field and Velet stripped a layer off the rug. In that went, too. Indulgently Old Al began a round:

"Red."

"Sun," said Pao-yu.

"The Red Sun Is," said one of the triplet Komarovs.

"The Red Sun Is—High," said Chi.

"The Red Sun Is High, The," Velet said.

"The Red Sun Is High, The Blue—"Jannina finished. They had come to Leslie Smith, who could either complete it or keep it going. She chose to declare for complete, not shyly (as before) but simply by pointing to Old Al.

"The red sun is high, the blue," he said. "Subtle! Another: Ching."

"Nü."

"Ching nü ch'i."

"Ching nü ch'i ch'u."

"Ssu."

"Wo."

"Ssu wo yü." It had got back to Leslie Smith again. She said, "I can't do that." Jannina got up and began to dance—I'm nice in my nasty way, she thought. The others wandered toward the pool and Ilse reappeared on the nursery monitor screen, saying, "I'm coming down." Somebody said, "What time is it in the Argentine?"

"Five A.M."

"I think I want to go."

"Go then."

"I go."

"Go well."

The red light over the antechamber door flashed and went out.

"Say, why'd you leave your other family?" said Ilse, settling near Old Al where the wall curved out. Ann, for whom it was evening, would be home soon: Chi, who had just got up a few hours back in western America, would stay somewhat longer; nobody ever knew Old Al's schedule and Jannina herself had lost track of the time. She would stay up until she felt sleepy. She followed a rough twenty-eight-hour day, Phuong (what a nuisance that must be at rehearsals!) a twenty-two-hour one, Ilse six hours up, six hours dozing. Jannina nodded, heard the question, and shook herself awake.

"I didn't leave them. They left me."

There was a murmur of sympathy around the pool.

"They left me because I was stupid," said Leslie Smith. Her hands were clasped passively in her lap. She looked very genteel in her blue body paint, a stocky young woman with small breasts. One of the triplet Komarovs, flirting in the pool with the other two, choked. The non-aquatic members of the family crowded around Leslie Smith, touching her with little, soft touches; they kissed her and exposed to her all their unguarded surfaces, their bellies, their soft skins. Old Al kissed her hands. She sat there, oddly unmoved. "But I *am* stupid," she said. "You'll find out." Jannina put her hands over her ears: "A masochist!" Leslie Smith looked at Jannina with a curious, stolid look. Then she looked down and absently began to rub one blue-painted knee. "Luggage!" shouted Chi, clapping his hands together, and the triplets dashed for the stairs. "No, I'm going to bed," said Leslie Smith; "I'm tired," and quite simply, she got up and let Old Al lead her through the pink room, the blue room, the turtle-and-pet room (temporarily empty), the trash room, and all the other rooms, to the guest room with the view that looked out over the cold hillside to the terraced plantings below.

"The best maker of hand-blown glass in the world," said Chi, "has killed in a duel the second-best maker of hand-blown glass in the world."

"For joining the movement to ceramics," said Ilse, awed. Jannina felt a thrill: this was the bitter stuff under the surface of life, the fury that boiled up. A bitter struggle is foreseen in the global economy. Good old tax-issue stuff goes toddling along, year after year. She was, thought Jannina, extraordinarily grateful to be living now, to be in such an extraordinary world, to have so long to go before her death. So much to do!

Old Al came back into the living room. "She's in bed."

"Well, which of us—?" said the triplet who-had-choked, looking mischievously round from one to the other. Chi was about to volunteer, out of his usual conscientiousness, thought Jannina, but then she found herself suddenly standing up, and then just as suddenly sitting down again. "I just don't have the nerve," she said. Velet Komarov walked on his hands toward the stairs, then somersaulted, and vanished, climbing. Old Al got off the hand-carved chest he had been sitting on and fetched a can of ale from it. He levered off the top and drank. Then he said, "She really is stupid, you know." Jannina's skin crawled.

"Oooh," said Pao-yu. Chi betook himself to the kitchen and returned with a paper folder. It was coated with frost. He shook it, then impatiently dropped it in the pool. The redheaded triplet swam over and took it. "Smith, Leslie," he said. "Adam Two, Leslie. Yee, Leslie Schwarzen, Leslie."

"What on earth does the woman *do* with herself besides get married?" exclaimed Pao-yu.

"She drove a hovercraft," said Chi, "in some out-of-the-way places around the Pacific until the last underground stations were completed. Says when she was a child she wanted to drive a truck."

175

"Well, you can," said the redheaded triplet, "can't you? Go to Arizona or the Rockies and drive on the roads. The sixty-mile-an-hour road. The thirty-mile-an-hour road. Great artistic recreation."

"That's not work," said Old Al.

"Couldn't she take care of children?" said the redheaded triplet. Ilse sniffed.

"Stupidity's not much of a recommendation for that," Chi said. "Let's see—no children. No, of course not. Overfulfilled her tax work on quite a few routine matters here. Kim, Leslie. Went to Moscow and contracted a double with some fellow, didn't last. Registered as a singleton, but that didn't last, either. She said she was lonely and they were exploiting her."

Old Al nodded.

"Came back and lived informally with a theater group. Left them. Went into psychotherapy. Volunteered for several experimental, intelligence-enhancing programs, was turned down—hm!—sixty-five come the winter solstice, muscular coordination average, muscular development above average, no overt mental pathology, empathy average, prognosis: poor. No, wait a minute, it says, 'More of the same.' Well, that's the same thing."

"What I want to know," added Chi, raising his head, "is who met Miss Smith and decided we needed the lady in this Ice Palace of ours?"

Nobody answered. Jannina was about to say, "Ann perhaps?" but as she felt the urge to do so—surely it wasn't right to turn somebody off like that, *just* for that!—Chi (who had been flipping through the dossier) came to the last page with the tax-issue stamp absolutely unmistakable, woven right into the paper.

"The computer did," said Pao-yu and she giggled idiotically.

"Well," said Jannina, jumping to her feet, "tear it up, my dear, or give it to me and I'll tear it up for you. I think Miss Leslie Smith deserves from us the same as we'd give to anybody else, and I—for one—intend to go *right up there—*"

"After Velet," said Old Al dryly.

"*With* Velet, if I must," said Jannina, raising her eyebrows, "and if you don't know what's due a guest, Old Daddy, I do, and I intend to provide it. Lucky I'm keeping house this month, or you'd probably feed the poor woman nothing but seaweed."

"You won't like her, Jannina," said Old Al.

"I'll find that out for myself," said Jannina with some asperity, "and I'd advise you to do the same. Let her garden with you, Daddy. Let her squirt the foam for the new rooms. And now"—she glared round at them—"I'm going to clean *this* room, so you'd better hop it, the lot of you," and dashing into the kitchen, she had the computer helmet on her head and the hoses going before they had even quite cleared the area of the pool. Then she took the helmet off and hung it on the wall. She flipped the cover off her wrist chronometer and satisfied herself as to the date. By the time she got back to the living room there was nobody there, only Leslie Smith's dossier lying on the carved chest. There was Leslie Smith; there was all of Leslie Smith. Jannina knocked on the wall cupboard and it revolved, presenting its openable side; she took out chewing gum. She started chewing and read about Leslie Smith.

Q: What have you seen in the last twenty years that you particularly liked?

A: I don't... the museum, I guess. At Oslo. I mean the... the mermaid and the children's museum, I don't care if it's a children's museum.

Q: Do you like children?

A: Oh no.

(No disgrace in *that*, certainly, thought Jannina.)

Q: But you liked the children's museum.

A: Yes, sir....Yes....I liked those little animals, the fake ones, in the—the—

Q: The crèche?

A: Yes. And I liked the old things from, the past, the murals with the flowers on them, they looked so real!

(Dear God!)

Q: You said you were associated with a theater group in Tokyo. Did you like it?

A: No...yes. I don't know.

Q: Were they nice people?

A: Oh yes. They were awfully nice. But they got mad at me, I suppose....You see...well, I don't seem to get things quite right, I suppose. It's not so much the work, because I do that all right, but the other... the little things. It's always like that.

Q: What do you think is the matter?

A: You...I think you know.

177

Jannina flipped through the rest of it: normal, normal, normal. Miss Smith was as normal as could be. Miss Smith was stupid. Not even very stupid. It was too damned bad. They'd probably have enough of Leslie Smith in a week, the Komarovs; yes, we'll have enough of her (Jannina thought), never able to catch a joke or a tone of voice, always clumsy, however willing, but never happy, never at ease. You can get a job for her, but what else can you get for her? Jannina glanced down at the dossier, already bored.

Q: You say you would have liked to live in the old days. Why is that? Do you think it would have been more adventurous or would you like to have had lots of children?

A: I ... you have no right ... You're condescending.

Q: I'm sorry. I suppose you mean to say that then you would have been of above-average intelligence. You would, you know.

A: I know. I looked it up. Don't condescend to me.

Well, it *was* too damned bad! Jannina felt tears rise in her eyes. What had the poor woman done? It was just an accident, that was the horror of it, not even a tragedy, as if everyone's forehead had been stamped with the word "Choose" except for Leslie Smith's. She needs money, thought Jannina, thinking of the bad old days when people did things for money. Nobody could take to Leslie Smith. She wasn't insane enough to stand for being hurt or exploited. She wasn't clever enough to interest anybody. She certainly wasn't feeble-minded; they couldn't very well put her into a hospital for the feeble-minded or the brain-injured; in fact (Jannina was looking at the dossier again) they had tried to get her to work there and she had taken a good, fast swing at the supervisor. She had said the people there were "hideous" and "revolting." She had no particular mechanical aptitudes. She had no particular interests. There was not even anything for her to read or watch; how could there be? She seemed (back at the dossier) to spend most of her time either working or going on public tours of exotic places, coral reefs and places like that. She enjoyed aqualung diving, but didn't do it often because that got boring. And that was that. There was, all in all, very little one could do for Leslie Smith. You might even say that in her own person she represented all the defects of the bad old days. Just imagine a world made up of such creatures! Jannina yawned. She slung the folder away and padded into the kitchen. Pity Miss Smith wasn't good-looking, also a pity that she was too well balanced (the folder said) to think that cosmetic surgery would make that much difference. Good for you, Leslie, you've got some sense, anyhow. Jannina, half asleep, met Ann in the kitchen, beautiful, slender Ann reclining on a cushion with her so-chi and melon. Dear old Ann. Jannina nuzzled her brown shoulder. Ann poked her.

"Look," said Ann, and she pulled from the purse she wore at her waist a tiny fragment of cloth, stained rusty brown.

"What's that?"

"The second-best maker of hand-blown glass—oh, you know about it—well, this is his blood. When the best maker of hand-blown glass in the world had stabbed to the heart the second-best maker of hand-blown glass in the world, and cut his throat, too, some small children steeped handkerchiefs in his blood and they're sending pieces all over the world."

"Good God!" cried Jannina.

"Don't worry, my dear," said lovely Ann; "it happens every decade or so. The children say they want to bring back cruelty, dirt, disease, glory, and hell. Then they forget about it. Every teacher knows that." She sounded amused. "I'm afraid I lost my temper today, though, and walloped your godchild. It's in the family, after all."

Jannina remembered when she herself had been much younger and Annie, barely a girl, had come to live with them. Ann had played at being a child and had put her head on Jannina's shoulder, saying, "Jannie, tell me a story." So Jannina now laid her head on Ann's breast and said, "Annie, tell me a story."

Ann said: "I told my children a story today, a creation myth. Every creation myth has to explain how death and suffering came into the world, so that's what this one is about. In the beginning, the first man and the first woman lived very contentedly on an island until one day they began to feel hungry. So they called to the turtle who holds up the world to send them something to eat. The turtle sent them a mango and they ate it and were satisfied, but the next day they were hungry again.

"'Turtle,' they said, 'send us something to eat.' So the turtle sent them a coffee berry. They thought it was pretty small, but they ate it anyway and were satisfied. The third day they called on the turtle again and this time the turtle sent them two things: a banana and a stone. The man and woman did not know which to choose, so they asked the turtle which thing it was they should eat. 'Choose,' said the turtle. So they chose the banana and ate that, but they used the stone for a game of catch. Then the turtle said, 'You should have chosen the stone. If you had chosen the stone, you would have lived forever, but now that you have chosen the banana, Death and Pain have entered the world, and it is not I that can stop them."

Jannina was crying. Lying in the arms of her old friend, she wept bitterly, with a burning sensation in her chest and the taste of death and ashes in her mouth. It was awful. It was horrible. She remembered the embryo shark she had seen when she was three, in the Auckland Cetacean Research Center, and how she had cried then. She didn't know what she was crying about."Don't, don't!" she sobbed.

"Don't what?" said Ann affectionately. "Silly Jannina!"

"Don't, don't," cried Jannina, "don't, it's true, it's true!" and she went on in this way for several more minutes. Death had entered the world. Nobody could stop it. It was ghastly. She did not mind for herself but for others, for her godchild, for instance. He was going to die. He was going to suffer. Nothing could help him. Duel, suicide, or old age, it was all the same. "This life!" gasped Jannina. "This awful life!" The thought of death became entwined somehow with Leslie Smith, in bed upstairs, and Jannina began to cry afresh, but eventually the thought of Leslie Smith calmed her. It brought her back to herself. She wiped her eyes with her hand. She sat up. "Do you want a smoke?" said beautiful Ann, but Jannina shook her head. She began to laugh. Really, the whole thing was quite ridiculous.

"There's this Leslie Smith," she said, dry-eyed. "We'll have to find a tactful way to get rid of her. It's idiotic, in this day and age."

And she told lovely Annie all about it.

SCIENCE FICTION BESTSELLERS
FROM BERKLEY

Frank Herbert

DUNE	(03698-7—$2.25)
DUNE MESSIAH	(03930-7—$1.95)
CHILDREN OF DUNE	(04075-5—$2.25)

Philip José Farmer

THE FABULOUS RIVERBOAT	(03793-2—$1.75)
TO YOUR SCATTERED BODIES GO	(03744-4—$1.75)
NIGHT OF LIGHT	(03933-1—$1.75)

Robert A. Heinlein

STRANGER IN A STRANGE LAND	(03782-7—$2.25)
THE MOON IS A HARSH MISTRESS	(03850-5—$1.95)
TIME ENOUGH FOR LOVE	(03471-2—$2.25)

Send for a list of all our books in print.

These books are available at your local bookstore, or send price indicated plus 30¢ for postage and handling. If more than four books are ordered, only $1.00 is necessary for postage. Allow three weeks for delivery. Send orders to:

Berkley Book Mailing Service
P.O. Box 690
Rockville Centre, New York 11570

IN 1918 AMERICA FACED AN ENERGY CRISIS

UNCLE SAM NEEDS THAT EXTRA SHOVELFUL

Help Uncle Sam to Win the War

An icy winter gripped the nation. Frozen harbors blocked the movement of coal. Businesses and factories closed. Homes went without heat. Prices skyrocketed. It was America's first energy crisis now long since forgotten, like the winter of '76-'77 and the oil embargo of '73-'74. Unfortunately, forgetting a crisis doesn't solve the problems that cause it. Today, the country is relying too heavily on foreign oil. That reliance is costing us over $40 billion dollars a year. Unless we conserve, the world will soon run out of oil, if we don't run out of money first. So the crises of the past may be forgotten, but the energy problems of today and tomorrow remain to be solved. The best solution is the simplest: conservation. It's something every American can do.

ENERGY CONSERVATION -
IT'S YOUR CHANCE TO SAVE, AMERICA

Department of Energy, Washington, D.C.

A PUBLIC SERVICE MESSAGE FROM BERKLEY PUBLISHING CO., INC.